SPAWN POINT

THE NEXTWORLD SERIES
BOOK TWO
JARON LEE KNUTH

SEVERED PRESS
HOBART TASMANIA

spawn point

ISBN: 978-1-925711-50-9

Also by Jaron Lee Knuth

After Life
Fixing Sam
Demigod
The Infinite Life of Emily Crane
Nottingham

The NextWorld Series

Level Zero
Spawn Point
End Code

The Super Power Saga

Super Powers of Mass Destruction
Rise of the Supervillains
Fear the Empire

"Whatever that be which thinks,
understands, wills, and acts.
It is something celestial and divine."

- Marcus Tullius Cicero

00101101

I won the game.

I killed my enemies and I got the girl.

You'd think I'd find contentment in the fact that with an army of Level Zeros, all operating at the same Level as me, I could kill every monster in every zone. The civilians are free to spend their days without fear, gathering information from every book the designers placed inside the world, learning and exploring their newfound emotions.

Yet here I am, marching the Level Zeros into another unfinished zone over the Darkfyre Mountains, continuing my search for more game to play. The name on the map is a series of meaningless numbers with multiple decimal points, but it's massive, four times the size of the desert zone. It's full of hills and valleys and clusters of trees, with a canyon that rips through the center, ending in a cliff side that falls off the edge of the world.

Every time we reach the top of another hill, a valley stretches out toward the horizon, mocking me with its emptiness. There are no structures, no signs of civilization or activity of any kind. There are only tall grasses swaying in the wind like waves of green. It's been weeks since we've entered the zone. The troops are growing restless, but not nearly as restless as me. I slide my pistols back into their holsters and let out a defeated sigh.

The barbarian standing next to me says, "It's the same thing." He pushes the blond hair out of his eyes and adjusts the horned helmet on his head, his arms flexing as he performs the simple task. "I'm starting to think Cyren is right. These zones beyond the Darkfyre Mountains were probably meant for some kind of future expansion, a planned area that wasn't finished by the time they released the beta."

"I'm not going to give up," I say, lifting my telescopic goggles to my eyes and zooming in on the next hill. "If there's something out there, we're going to find it."

"Forgive him," a voice from behind us says. "Arkade is annoyed that he's run out of things to kill."

We both turn to see Cyren climbing up to meet us. Her black leather straps glisten in the sunlight, every metal buckle twinkling like a star against the night sky that is her body. Her arms lift her lithe body without any effort as she hops onto the boulder next to me. When she leans over to hug me, her black lips brush against my cheek, planting a kiss as they pass.

"I'm not just trigger-happy," I say, even though it's a lie. "We need to know if there are any monsters left. I'm not going to rest until there's nothing left to threaten the life of any NPC."

"As you've said many times before." Cyren flashes a knowing smile. "But there's something you don't understand."

"No? What's that?"

"There will always be the threat of death for us. Car accidents, natural disasters... heck, I could fall off this boulder right now and snap my neck."

"As long as the Level Zeros are grouped with me, their Levels will match my Level 100. You're not going to suffer much damage falling from this height."

Cyren smirks, like she thinks my argument is cuter than it is poignant.

"You're missing the point. That impending doom? That fear of death? That makes us more human."

"It helps us understand you," the barbarian says as he slaps my back, knocking me forward with his Level 100 strength. "From what I've read, fear is the source of most human interactions."

"We should get moving," I say, pointing toward the nearby hilltop. "We could reach the next hill by nightfall."

The barbarian points to the western sky. "There's a storm coming. We should make camp."

"We still have time to—"

"No," Cyren says firmly, "*we* don't. Because *we* have a previous engagement."

I take off my cowboy hat, knocking the dust from the brim. "We do?"

"Xen and Raev?"

"Oh. Right. Of course. I—"

"You forgot."

"No. I just..."

"It's okay. If I didn't expect you to forget, I wouldn't know you very well," she says with that same comforting smile. "But these are your best friends. I think it might be nice not to be late to their partnership ceremony."

"Fine," I say with a pouted bottom lip, but when I turn around to give orders to the barbarian, I stand up straight. "Send the scouts ahead of us. I want them to reach that tree line and report back before daybreak."

The barbarian nods and makes his way down the hill, back toward our camp.

"Don't look so depressed," Cyren says, playfully punching my arm. "The Omniversalist partnership ceremony is a celebration." When I don't respond, she adds, "That means you should smile."

I know she's calling me out, so I force a chuckle. "Sorry. It's just that... I mean, Xen and I barely get a chance to talk anymore. And it's not my fault this time! He's been so busy with Raev and getting everything organized..."

"You should be excited to see him then."

"Yeah. Maybe."

"Do you have a speech prepared?"

The size of my eyes reveal how startled I am by the question. "A speech? I have to give a speech?"

Cyren slaps my arm, less playfully this time. "Of course you do! You're his witness!"

"No one told me that involved talking to people!"

"It's common knowledge."

"Not common enough, apparently."

Cyren tugs on my arm, leading me down the hill, back toward the camp. "Come on. I'll help you write something."

"Can't I just... wing it?"

"This isn't a low Level quest. You're going to be in front of a crowd, and they're going to expect you to at least pretend you feel emotional about your friend's happiness."

"Seriously?"

"Seriously."

"Don't you think this ceremony is... kind of pointless?"

"When you say things like that, it proves that there is no way I'm going to let you 'wing it.'"

"I thought Omniversalism was all about telling the truth," I say with a smirk. "The truth is, I think this is kind of pointless."

"That isn't funny. This day is important to Xen and Raev, and you should be honored you're a part of it."

I grunt, pretending to acknowledge what she's saying, but Cyren doesn't let me off the hook.

"What's the problem now?"

I bite my lip, knowing I shouldn't say anything, but of course it comes out anyway. "It's just that people are always telling me how I *should* feel, but it's never how I actually feel."

"And by people, do you mean me?"

I shrug my shoulders and mumble, "Sometimes."

She grabs on to my wrist and stops my descent down the hill. She yanks harder and pulls me so close to her that I'm looking into her eyes from a few inches away.

"I'm trying to help you."

"I know," I say, my eyes shifting from side to side, looking at everything except her.

She appears more sullen than before as she says, "I'm trying to help myself too."

My eyes flash to her.

She turns away from me and looks out over the camp of Level Zeros. "As more and more connections are forming in our programming, we're becoming more like you. These feelings, these emotions—we're experiencing them for the first time. Some of us aren't sure how to deal with it. Some of us get overwhelmed. But you have this lock on everything you're feeling, like you can control your emotions, set them aside so you can focus on logic and reason."

"Is that what you think I'm doing? You think I'm controlling my emotions?"

She glances over her shoulder with eyes so sad that I want to reach out and hold her and tell her everything will be all right, even if I'm lying.

"I don't know, Arkade. Sometimes I think the more I feel, the less I understand."

I can't help laughing to myself. "Cyren... sometimes I think you and the other NPCs are becoming more human than I will ever be."

But I'm lying again. I don't think Cyren and the other Level Zeros are becoming more human. I think they're becoming something else entirely.

00101110

When we sit down to watch the video-cast of Xen and Raev's partnership ceremony, I realize how nice it is to have some time with Cyren. It's rare to share quiet moments with her. I'm always moving forward, over the next hill, looking for more of the game. Holding her hand, with her head on my shoulder, is a treasure I never stop craving.

The screen playing the video-cast is hovering in front of us. Cyren can't access casts from outside of the game world, so I try to explain everything that's happening.

Xen looks happy. Happier than I've ever seen him look. His smile is beaming like the sun itself. The moment Raev enters the room, he looks like he might explode. She's wearing a plain gray cloth wrapped around her body multiple times, per Omniversalist tradition, but it looks nice against the deep blue of her avatar's skin. Her hair looks like rainbow-colored ribbons that stream behind her as if there was a constant gust of wind blowing through the room. As she approaches, her eyes never leave Xen. They're lost in each other.

From the back of the church, a DJ plays music. He mixes their two favorite songs together to create something that sounds entirely new. Cyren assures me this is symbolic.

Even though she can't see it, the whole ceremony is making her cry. She keeps apologizing for it and I keep telling her it's okay, but it scares me. It's affecting her on a level I'm afraid I won't ever understand. To me it looks unnecessarily decadent.

As the ceremony continues, Cyren explains the details of the ritual to me. Omniversalism is one of the things she's been studying, trying to understand the human need for spirituality. She's tried talking to me about her theories of souls and binary code, but I spend most of the conversation nodding my head. That stuff has never felt important to me. It's like a puzzle with a solution that holds no reward. What's the point?

The Omniversalist teacher reads from some ancient text called "First Origins" before lighting a series of candles. Each candle emits a different colored flame.

"Why eleven?" I ask, trying to appear intrigued.

"Each one represents a quality of partnership that they should honor."

I can't help smirking. "Only eleven? That doesn't sound so hard."

Cyren elbows me in the ribs. "Be nice."

"And what's this about?" I ask, trying to restrain my reaction to the spectacle. "Why are there white feathers falling from the sky? It looks like a blizzard."

"It symbolizes the purity and weightlessness of love."

"Of course it does."

Cyren wipes the tears from her eyes, leans away from me, and crosses her leather-strapped arms over her chest. "You can resist this all you want, but I've seen you be romantic before."

"Romance? Sure. I just don't think it needs to be this complicated. I love you, but I don't need magic or spirits or any of that stuff to explain it. It's more logical to me."

"Oh really?" she says, leaning forward, suddenly very interested in what I'm saying. "Perhaps you'd care to explain the logic of romance?"

This isn't the conversation I want to be having, but I see on the video-cast that the Omniversalist teacher is changing his robes into a waterfall that is cascading down the front of the church and washing over the audience. Whatever that's supposed to symbolize is even less interesting to me.

"When I met you, you were the first person I felt like I could relate to. Ever. You were uncomfortable around people. I saw every moment that you were trying to pretend to fit in with them. I knew what you were doing because I was doing the same thing."

She smiles and says, "So you love me because I'm just like you?"

"No," I say with frustration, but I'm only frustrated with my own inability to explain myself. "That's how I felt when I met you, but as we spent more time together, I realized how much we complemented each other. Your strengths are my weaknesses, and vice versa. My logic is your emotion. My calculated response is your brazen action. My ranged attack is your melee."

She lets out a chuckle. "My melee? Coming from anyone else, that might be the strangest compliment ever given. But from you? That's the sweetest thing you've ever said."

"I'm trying to say that for me, love isn't just something I feel. It isn't some unquantifiable emotion. Love is something I do. It's a physical action. It's a verb, not a noun. I *love* you. Whether that's through a simple kiss, or holding a door open for you, or protecting you from that giant praying mantis."

"Yeah. Thanks again for that. It would have been a terrible way to die."

"I love you because you're the greatest person I've ever known."

She closes her eyes and bows her head, hearing my words as deeply as she can before leaning in and kissing me. I want the moment to last longer, but out of the corner of my eye I notice something happening on the screen.

Both Xen and Raev's chests burst open, a golden chain springing forth and locking together in the middle. As I explain the bizarre image to Cyren, she responds more calmly than I expect.

"Their hearts are to remain bound to each other for the rest of the night."

"That's... grotesque."

The Omniversalist teacher bellows through the church in his most commanding voice, "I now pronounce the souls of these two partners forever locked in the space of infinity!"

The crowd cheers. I consciously watch everyone's reaction as Xen and Raev parade through the audience, shaking hands and hugging people. Xen points right at our camera and waves at me. Cyren urges me to wave back.

The camera follows the couple into the adjoining room for the celebration of their partnership. I settle in and summon all the mental strength I have in my body, knowing this is the part of the day where I'll have to interact with people. I lean over and grip Cyren's hand for support, but we're interrupted when someone throws open the entrance to our tent.

The barbarian steps into the room, his hands pulling aside the curtains of blond hair washing across his shoulders. Each strand curls at the end with a sort of playfulness that's ironic compared to the rest of his violent physique.

"Sorry to interrupt," he says, "but we found something."

I jump to my feet, trying uselessly to hide my excitement at the sudden turn toward the game world. Cyren jumps up next to me and pushes me back down on to my chair.

"You're not going anywhere."

"But—"

"You have a speech to give," she says, pointing her leather-gloved finger right in my face. "We're all Level 100. I think we'll be able to handle whatever this is. I'll be back as soon as I can, but in case I don't make it in time, I want you to record your speech with your in-game camera so I can watch it later."

"But—"

"Stay," she says, wiggling her finger again. Then she leans down, kisses my cheek, and whispers, "You'll do great."

Her kiss takes my breath away long enough for her to leave the tent without any more argument. The cloth door closes as they begin to discuss whatever exciting things are happening in the zone. I let out a long, dramatic breath and cross my arms in my best pouting form.

There's more. I knew it. More zones to explore, more monsters to kill, more game to play.

I try to summon a look of attentiveness as I watch the entire audience of Xen and Raev's family and friends file into the celebration room of the church, but even without a golden chain, my heart and my mind are with Cyren. Always.

00101111

I can't stop thinking about what the Level Zeros have found, but I try to bring myself back to the moment I'm experiencing.

"Xen is my best friend," I say into the screen.

The crowd in the celebration room is staring back at me. A sea of faces hang on my every word. I know the palms of my hands are sweating in the real world, but my avatar looks calm and collected. I hope.

"You might not think that's a big deal, seeing as how I only have one friend, but that's exactly why it's important. There aren't many people who could put up with somebody like me."

The crowd laughs. They think I'm joking.

"Most people think I'm so self-absorbed that it wouldn't be possible for me to care about anyone else. It takes a special person to look past my exterior. I have an obnoxious inability to interact with anyone. At least using anything other than my awkward social skills. I often indulge in a distanced analyzing of other people. I have idiosyncratic, nuanced behavioral disabilities. I mean, what I'm trying to say is that most of the time I'm a real jerk."

The crowd isn't laughing anymore. They're shuffling in their seats. Someone clears their throat, making the silence more obvious.

"My point is, Xen has always been able to look past that. He ignores the avatar and sees the person that lies within. For every failure, he sees a success to match it. He tells me that this is what Omniversalism teaches us to do, but that doesn't mean we all do it. It takes someone special, someone like Xen, to excel so highly at being a good person."

I smile, more to myself than anyone else, because I know I'm almost done. I've almost completed the task. Soon the attention will be off of me and I'll be able to breathe again.

"Luckily for Raev, there isn't anything to look past. She's a beautiful, thoughtful person, and I have no trouble seeing why Xen would choose her to partner with. I'm sure it's just as obvious to everyone gathered here today. So without any trepidation, I'd like to congratulate them both for finding a perfect partner with whom to travel through this life."

The crowd cheers. It's almost like no one noticed how terrified I was. Or no one cared. Maybe they're as happy that I'm done as I am. I try to remind myself that maybe this moment isn't about me. I was just a momentary distraction from the real spectacle.

Xen and Raev stand up and they share a kiss for all to see. The crowd loves it, their cheers growing louder. I pull my screen to the back of the room, relaxing into the shadows where no one will notice me. The awkward weight lifts from me as the thousand eyes look away. I can breathe.

There is a procession of congratulations. A line of people wait to shake hands with Xen and Raev and offer brief points of partnership advice. Some share humorous anecdotes from the past, others give a simple word that sums up the attractiveness of the ceremony.

I watch from the back of the room, trying to wrap my brain around why anyone would partake in such a strangely choreographed ritual in order to exemplify their relationship for others. I've never felt the need to explain what Cyren means to me. Not even to her. She understands. That's one of the things that's so great about her.

As NPCs pass plates and serving trays full of glowing food and colored drinks around the room, I notice Xen and Raev stand from their throne-like chairs at the head of the room and make their way through the crowd. People stop them to chat and tell Raev how beautiful she looks, but soon enough they smile and wave their hands at my screen.

"Kade!" Xen says through his still-beaming smile, rocking back and forth on the heels of his feet, barely able to contain himself.

"Hi," I say, limply waving my hand at the screen. "Um... congratulations."

"Thanks," Raev says. "You did good."

I shrug my shoulders. "I'm just glad it's over. I hate doing stuff like that."

Raev chuckles, unsure if I'm joking or not.

Xen clears his throat. "Either way, we're glad you're here."

I reply with a single word: "Cool."

I wish Cyren was here. She always knows how to fill the gaps in conversations.

Before I can think of anything to say, a hand reaches out from the corner of the screen and grabs Raev's arm. An older woman steps into view, her rigid face looking anything but happy. There's nothing unique about her design, but I can tell she's from an elite line of avatars. It's a very boring, very expensive model for the business-conscious user that doesn't want to make a statement other than "I can afford to be a conformist."

"I would like to speak with you."

Raev runs her hand along the golden chain bound to Xen's heart and says with an authoritative voice, "My partner and I are talking with our friend right now. We'll let you know when we're done."

The woman squints her eyes and inhales through her nose, holding on to Raev's arm for a long moment before releasing her grip and storming off into the crowd.

"What was that about?"

Raev runs her free hand through the rainbow ribbons on her head, straightening them before releasing them to flow freely over her shoulder. With a deep breath, her sarcastic attitude returns.

"That was my mother. The life of the party."

"Raev's mother isn't exactly thrilled about our partnership," Xen says, his smile looking weak and forced.

"Oh, that's not true," Raev says with a sardonic smile. "Our partnership doesn't bother her. It's my choice to join you in DOTgod that really stokes her fire."

"I take it she isn't religious?" I ask, surprised by my own interest.

It's possible that I'm feeling something akin to empathy for Raev. I understand the disappointment of a parent when you refuse to follow the path they've laid out for you.

"It's more than her philosophical differences with Omniversalism. She owns InfoLock. It's one of the biggest information insurance companies in NextWorld. Her success provided us with financial security and gave me opportunities that, I can't deny, were pretty extraordinary. The fact that she was able to get a child license as a single mother should tell you how much influence she can throw around."

DOTgov looks past a lot of their own rules when you have enough credits.

"But she expected you to take over the family business, not join a religious movement," I say, filling in the rest of the story from my own experience.

"She's been grooming me for InfoLock since I was a child. She used her money to give me the best of everything, but she also used that same money to control my life."

The design of Raev's avatar is quite amazing. And expensive. The detail doesn't hide the tension in her face. She clenches her teeth and tightens her jaw.

"She dangles her credits over my head like she's trying to teach a new trick to her pet."

"So you're saying that joining up with a humble, minimalistic religion wouldn't exactly thrill her?"

Raev laughs boisterously, trying to step away from her own seriousness. "You should have seen my mother's face when I told her that the church pays for the ceremony." She lifts the back of Xen's hand toward her lips, laying a soft kiss upon it. "But it doesn't matter. None of it. I've found my partner. I've found love. That's all I need."

They get lost in each other's gaze again, but this time I'm not as disgusted by the display. In fact, I begin to feel something, a connection to what they're experiencing, when the game announcer's booming voice breaks in.

"Group member Devyl has died."

"Group member Alfa has died."

"Group member Phaet has died."

"Group member Newk has died."

"Group member Saynt has died."

"Group member Epek has died."

"Group member Taifoon has died."

"Group member Dedhed has died."

I'm forced to turn off the alerts as an emergency voice-cast from Cyren appears in the corner of my view.

I slam my hand on to the icon and hear her voice shouting over a thunderous roar of gunfire and magic spells.

"I shouldn't be sending you this, I shouldn't be asking you to do this, but we don't have a choice. I need your help."

I'm standing up from the couch before I'm aware of what's happening. Xen and Raev don't have a chance to react before I'm pulling out my revolvers and checking to see which advanced ammunition I have selected.

"What's going on?" Xen asks. "Is there trouble?"

"Yes," I say, my hands shaking as I select different options in the menu. "Something is... I don't know..."

"Cyren?" Raev asks.

I nod my head, unable to say the words.

Raev leans in closer to the screen. "Go to her."

I nod my head again, acknowledging the fact that she understands how dire the situation is.

"Let us know what happens," Xen manages to say right before I swipe my hand to close the screen.

I throw open the flap and step into an empty camp. The Level Zeros are gone. I open my map and see the cluster of dots that represent my group a few miles away. I climb the side of the hill and open my list of magic items with a single gesture of my hand. I select my default load-out: Anti-Gravity Belt, Boots of Leaping, and Ring of Magic Protection. I use the boots to launch off the rocky cluster at the top of the hill and as I plummet toward the valley below, I activate my Anti-Gravity Belt and land softly on the grass. My feet pound against the soil, pushing me as fast as possible toward my goal. Toward the only thing that matters.

Cyren.

00110000

As I reach the tree line that I ordered my scouts to search, the vegetation manages to block out what is left of the dwindling sunlight. A twisting maze of trails wind through the trees, but as I get closer, I don't need the map to direct me toward Cyren. I just follow the rattle of gunfire and the rumble of explosions. The sounds make my heart beat faster. My hands clench my pistols tighter. I don't want to admit how excited I am, but I can't deny it.

When I reach the scene of the battle, I launch myself from the thick curtain of vines into a clearing. I try to take in my surroundings, but the chaos overwhelms me for a moment. Winged demons explode in the open air as a sniper team fires from the cover of the tree line. Flashes of gun barrels join the blinding lights of various magic spells. Screams of rage from the Level Zeros are followed by screams of pain from the demons they're fighting.

High walls encircle a courtyard with a single, crooked tower in the middle, rising toward the sky. The ancient temple rests in the center of the clearing, twisted and evil in its architectural complexity. The stone is black with moisture, wrapped by vines and natural growth trying to cover its shameful existence. Green moss fills every crack, decaying as it reaches toward the top of the tower. A flash of lightning streaks down from the peak, striking a group of

Level Zeros advancing toward the front doors. The demons bubble out of large cracks in the ground like a gelatinous liquid of horrifying crimson flesh. Nothing more than clumps of gnashing teeth and writhing tentacles, they eventually separate into smaller, misshapen creatures. Some take to the air, their tiny wings flapping furiously, trying to keep their bodies aloft.

I raise the barrel of my pistol, aiming it at the demon flying in the center of the flock. My eyes squint, my teeth clench, my trigger finger flexes, and with a single gunshot I'm playing the game again.

I pop off a few more rounds and find myself disgusted when the bulbous bodies explode into demonic goo. It's been a long time since I've seen violence in the game. Too long.

I hold down my triggers, using the automatic gunfire upgrade I purchased to wave the streams of bullets through the sky, cutting through more and more of the horrible creatures. I only stop when I see Cyren slamming her foot into the head of one demon while breaking the neck of another. I sprint toward her.

"What is this place?" I shout as I leap over the bodies of the demons piling up around her.

She drops the corpse of another demon and glances up at me. I can't tell what the look on her face means. She's either relieved to see me, or she's more scared now that I'm here.

"There's no end to them," she yells over the shotgun firing next to us. "They just keep multiplying. We've got to end this before they outnumber us."

I remember a quest from when I was first playing the game. The quest where I met Fantom. There were aliens that acted the same way. They kept coming, a never-ending source of enemies.

"There's something we need to destroy, an item of some kind," I shout over the crackle of an ice spell that freezes five demons overhead. They fall to the ground and shatter into pieces. "And whatever we have to destroy is most likely in that temple."

"That's why I contacted you," she says as the temple releases a bolt of lighting, striking another group of Level Zeros. "We can't get near that thing without it blasting us. We've got nothing to protect ourselves from lightning magic. But you have—"

"The Mirror Shield," I say, finishing her sentence.

I swipe my hand in the air to open my inventory of magic items, scrolling through pages and pages until I find the reward I got for killing the Medusa boss in the secret labyrinth underneath the desert. The Mirror Shield appears on my arm, the sun shining off its reflective surface.

I lock my mind back into my gamer thought patterns. "Keep these things occupied. I'll take care of the tower."

"Nice try," she says, stepping next to me and punching her fist through the head of a demon swooping down at us. "That shield is big enough to protect both of us, and whatever is inside that temple might require more than one Level 100 player."

I open my mouth to respond, but she continues: "If you thought I was going to let you run off by yourself—"

"I wouldn't dream of it," I say with a smile, feeling the nostalgia of having her by my side in battle again.

She leans in, inches from my ear, and whispers, "Let's go to work."

I want to correct her. I want to remind her that this is fun. I want to remind her that this is a game. We're not going to work. We're going to play. But I know she disagrees. We're here for a reason. These monsters threaten the safety of me, the Level Zeros, and the civilians.

With the other Level Zeros fighting alongside us, we force our way through the torrential rise of demons, battling our way through a wall of mouths and talons and wings. Snipers take down every demon flapping above us in the sky. Heads explode, limbs break free, and the swing of a sword or the crushing blow of a hammer silence the few that land on the ground.

My own gunshots join the swarm of bullets and arrows from the ranged team. We lay waste to row after row of the misshapen creatures. The jagged hooks of medieval weaponry tear the bodies asunder, gargantuan clubs splatter them across the courtyard floor, and the razor sharp edges of twirling blades carve the demons into pieces. Elemental magic sparkles and twists through the air, destroying each demon with blocks of ice, walls of fire, spinning tornadoes, and giant boulders. Yet as each demon falls to their doom, another red body emerges from the ground to fill their ranks.

As we near the main entrance to the temple, a cluster of demons erupts from the ground, completely blocking our path. Cyren leaps into action before I can react, becoming a spinning vortex of hard limbs. She shatters bones and launches bodies across the courtyard with her Level 100 strength. Her dance of death is stunning, and I find myself lost in its beauty for a moment. Just long enough for two demons to tackle me to the ground.

00110001

The creature on my chest leans in, hissing into my face. Its silver teeth drip with acidic ooze as its mouth opening wide to devour me. The Mirror Shield is the only thing holding its gaping maw at bay. I turn my face away from the burning saliva that is slowly dropping from the demon's mouth, but I can still hear the clicking of its gnashing teeth.

The other creature has decided to work its way up from the bottom. A tentacle wraps itself around my leg right before rows of razor sharp fangs sink into my thigh. The teeth hit bone, my knee cap cracks under the power of its jaw, and I find myself wishing the coding of the pain in this game wasn't so real. I try to kick at the demon, but at the difficulty rating of these demons, my melee attacks are harmless.

I chose guns for a reason.

I dislodge one of my pistols from underneath the demon on top of me and shove the barrel into the face that's eating my leg. A quick pull of the trigger and the source of my pain turns into a cloud of red scales.

Trying to hold back the demon on my shield with only one arm proves impossible. As the demon's mouth opens to ravage my entire face, it's thrown from my body, squealing in pain as it flies through the air. I look up and see the content smile of a barbarian shining through his blond hair.

"If I stole that kill from you, I apologize," he says, offering me his free hand to help me from the ground.

I accept his help and as soon as I get to my feet, I take a shot at a demon swooping overhead. "There will be plenty more kills to be had for the both of us."

He nods and says, "Aye," as he clutches his large wooden club with both hands and rushes toward a cluster of demons.

I look out over the heads of everyone on the battlefield. The Level Zeros are holding fast, decimating the demonic forces as quickly as they're birthed from the ground, but we aren't making any headway. It's a violent standstill.

"We aren't getting any closer to the tower entrance," Cyren shouts over the clash of weaponry all around us. "All we're accomplishing is a steady increase to our kill ratings."

I take a shot at another demon. Its head explodes and its body topples to the ground. I bring my mind back to a time when I used to command these Level Zeros in battle rather than just pushing them forward into empty territories.

"Arrow formation. Break a line through the battle. You and I will split the middle."

She holds up a fist in the air, raises two fingers from her fist, and the melee team moves into position. The mass of fighters create a pointed V directly toward the entrance, pushing the demons outward as they advance. Cyren and I charge forward, down the center of the V, toward the point of their formation.

I'm hobbling on my wounded leg, trying to keep up with Cyren, when a demon breaks through the formation. Before he's able to attack, Cyren leaps into the air, rolling over the demon and kicking backward. Her leather heel caves in the demon's skull.

As we reach the tip of the formation, the fighters split open, allowing us to break free and sprint toward the entrance. The lightning magic bursts from the top of the tower, but my Mirror Shield is already in position. The magic reflects off the surface and arcs away from us in a random direction, striking a group of demons rising from the cracked courtyard. Their electrified corpses turn black as they crumple to the ground. Our melee team fills in the gap behind us, blocking the demons from following us into the temple and giving us time to infiltrate the ancient structure.

When we reach the stone entrance, Cyren lowers one shoulder. The ancient rock crumbles under her momentum and we rush into the foyer of the temple. The damp, black walls curve overhead with crooked angles and twisted beams supporting the upper levels. Dust and pebbles fall from the ceiling as the clash of battle echoes from outside. The faces of ancient gods are carved into pillars throughout the open area, their eyes glowing red with an unholy purpose. I hear the screech of a bat, then something that sounds like a low rumble in the distance. It takes me a second before I realize its laughter.

"Creepy," Cyren says before she takes a step toward the center of the room.

When she does, I look down at the floor and notice hieroglyphic symbols carved into the stone. Her foot touches one and it begins to glow. My hand lashes out, grabbing on to her shoulder. As I yank her back, a buzz saw swings down from the ceiling, the blade passing inches from her face.

She swallows hard and says, "Thank you."

I point to the symbols on the floor. "Standard evil temple stuff. I've seen it in a thousand games."

She glances out the doorway at the bloodshed still exploding in the courtyard. "We don't have time to critique the level design right now."

I blink once and turn away. "Right. Sorry."

I carefully step through the maze of symbols, only placing my foot on unmarked stone, planning four or five steps ahead. There's only one way to get through the symbols, even though it looks like there's a hundred, so if I don't think ahead, I end up having to backtrack. We don't have that kind of time.

Cyren follows my every footstep, placing her trust in my gameplay. There is no doubt in her allegiance. We know each others' strengths and weaknesses, and we know how to compliment both. Xen would call it Yin and Yang. We prefer to call it binary. One and Zero. With a sum that's greater than its parts. We are a team. Now and forever.

After dodging a few spear traps on the way up the staircase, we find the next level covered in flowing lava. Chains dangle from the ceiling, allowing us to swing between stone platforms. Apparently Cyren can read my reaction to the room from my facial expression.

"Still not satisfied?" Cyren asks.

"Lava?" I let out a breath of derision. "I mean, come on. It's the second floor of the temple. How did lava get up here? It's sloppy design."

With a single leap she latches on to a chain and maneuvers between platforms. I activate my Boots of Leaping and cover the room in three bounds.

When Cyren catches up to me on the other side, she steps past me with a smirk and says, "Show off."

"Hey," I call after her, hurrying up the staircase to the next floor. "It's not my fault that the game doesn't allow Level Zeros to use magic items."

The third floor is designed like some sort of cultist worship room. The ceiling is the interior of a twisted cone, reaching all the way to the top of the tower. At the front of the room, past a long, deteriorated carpet, stands a huge stone statue of an evil god towering over us. The head of a cobra stares down at us, its body carved with six arms, each holding a different item: a sword, a crescent moon-shaped hook, a lantern, a five-pointed star, an orb, and a hammer. Cyren stands by my side, waiting for my move. I study each object in the statue's hands.

"Well?" she asks. "Now what?

As if on cue, the stone statue of the evil god creaks and groans as the stone begins to move. I remove both of my pistols from their holsters.

"Finally. Something interesting."

Cyren looks around, worried. The six arms of the statue fan out like weaponized wings that are stretching for the first time in centuries. One of the hands throws the orb into the air. The stone sphere streaks up toward the top of the spiral roof, crackling with a glowing energy. It fills the entire room with a strange purple hue that hangs like dust in the air. The light of the orb flickers, casting shadows on the walls that dance with their own twisted merriment.

"What is that thing?" Cyren whispers, clenching her fists and digging her feet into the ground.

I raise my guns, taking careful aim as I smile. "It's a boss fight."

00110010

I activate my Boots of Leaping and my Anti-Gravity belt, launching myself into the air and holding down the triggers on both of my pistols. I hover through the room, unleashing a steady stream of bullets into the face of the statue. Chips of stone spray into the air, but the statue strides forward, unaffected.

The arm holding the sword swings at me. I pull my knees to my chest and flip forward. As the blade passes under me, I push off the flat edge with my good leg and rocket higher into the air, still shooting.

The arm that wields the hammer swings toward Cyren. She cartwheels to the side and the weapon crushes the ground behind her, leaving a crater in its wake. Cyren sprints toward the edge of the room. The arm with the five-pointed star reels back, then flings the shape toward her. She ducks and the star slams into the wall, one point embedding itself deep into the black stone. Cyren continues forward, running straight up the wall. Ten feet up, she pushes off, flipping backward. Her body tumbles through the air like a stiff baton until she spreads her limbs and lands upon the hand that threw the star at her.

I'm falling slowly. My bullets keep chipping away. The statue's cobra face looks mutilated, but there are no weak spots underneath. Just more stone. So I keep shooting.

As Cyren runs up the arm, the statue scrapes the crescent-shaped hook down the surface of its bicep, trying to remove her from its body. She leaps into the air and the hook passes underneath her. When she lands on the shoulder, she clenches both of her fists and raises them above her head. I can see her muscles bulge underneath the black straps of leather. She screams as her fists swing down like bombs and the impact creates a blast that turns the stone into a cloud of dust. She's lost inside the fog for a moment before she drops out of the bottom. With the shoulder completely disintegrated, the arm falls free, crashing to the ground and breaking into more pieces that scatter across the floor.

My bloody leg wobbles when I land, but my trigger fingers are still flexed. I dodge to the side as the statue swings the sword at me again. This time the blade cleaves into the ground, sticking for a moment. I turn both guns toward the fingers wrapped around the handle of the sword. The stone is thinner there. My guns chew through the hard surface and the thumb breaks free. When the statue yanks on the sword, its arm raises, but the sword remains stuck. The statue flexes its four remaining fingers in front of its face, confused by its inability to grip the weapon.

With two of its appendages rendered useless, I focus my shots at the arm that's wielding the hammer, considering it the next biggest threat. I'm wrong. The statue turns the lantern toward me and a beam of light surges from the interior. It hits me square in the chest before I can react. I'm thrown backward and my body crashes into a stone column that breaks, crumbling down on top of me.

I try to collect my thoughts and lift myself from the debris. My chest is burning. I look down and the area where the lantern struck me is still glowing, smoldering from the heat. It's possible that I'd be dead if it wasn't for my Ring of Magic Protection.

As soon as I look up, the lantern strikes me again. This time I hit the wall, which crumples under the impact. I hang there for a moment before tumbling out of the body-shaped crater and falling to my knees.

My ring can only protect me for so long. I can't risk another shot. I don't waste time checking my wounds this time. I roll to the side just as the beam strikes the spot where I was. I manage to get my feet underneath me and sprint the other way, zigzagging through the room, dodging the beam of light as it burns the floor behind me, searching for its target. It's moving faster than I can. The heat closes in on me, nipping at my heels.

Cyren slides underneath the statue's legs. She places a palm on the ankle and pulls back her other fist. Another explosive hit, a cloud of powdered stone, and the statue tumbles to the side. The lantern light streams to the side, away from me.

When the statue hits the floor, the entire room shakes. I'm almost thrown from my feet, but I manage to remain standing. The arms of the statue spread out to the sides, as its entire body flattens along the floor. Its foot remains standing, disconnected from the body at the ankle. Cyren stands next to it, her black leather covered in gray soot.

Using my Boots of Leaping, I push against the floor, launching myself on top of the statue. I land on its neck and point both of my pistols at the back of its head. The pointblank shots pound against the stone like a thousand jackhammers. I'm blinded by the large grains of dust that envelop me, but I keep shooting, stopping only when I feel a hand touch my shoulder.

The sound of gunfire echoes through the chamber for a few seconds after I stop shooting. Then there is silence. The cloud of dust drifts to the floor, leaving Cyren and I covered in gray, standing on the broken ruins of a dead god.

"We won," Cyren says, but there's no triumph in her voice. It sounds more like a question than a declaration of success.

I look up, toward the tip of the ceiling, and see the purple orb still crackling with energy.

"I thought that killing the statue would end the magical effect. Maybe we have to destroy the orb as well?"

I lift my pistol and take aim, but Cyren places her hand on my arm and lowers it.

"I've got a better idea," she says as she hops off the back of the statue and sprints toward the wall where the five-pointed star is stuck. She grips on to one of the points and pulls. The muscles in her arms ripple like waves of water, summoning as much of her Level 100 strength as she can. Cracks in the wall arc out from the point piercing the stone. With a final bellow of effort, the star breaks free. Cyren stumbles backward a few steps, barely able to hold the star aloft, yet when she spins in the middle of the room, the momentum allows her to twirl the star around in a circular arc. The points whirl past me, increasing in speed with each turn, until she tilts the star upward and releases it. The five points streak through the air, shooting straight for the orb.

When the star strikes the orb, there's a flash of purple light that burns my retinas. A warmth cascades over my body. As the light fades, it leaves the temple room dark. Through the thick stone of the temple walls I can hear cheers from the Level Zeros outside. I slide both pistols into my holsters and let out a long, heavy breath, finally allowing my muscles to relax. My shoulders slump forward and I take off my hat, running my fingers through my hair as if I'm physically telling my brain it can slow down. It can stop analyzing movement and speed and velocity. It can let go of its stranglehold on strategy.

We accomplished our goal.

We won.

I'm about to call out to Cyren to congratulate her when I hear a rumble from above. A rain of dust falls down upon me. Then a stone. A rock. A large chunk of the ceiling crashes into the floor next to me. I look up at Cyren, but she's already next to me, grabbing on to my arm and yanking me toward the staircase. We run, leaping down three and four steps at a time.

When we reach the floor below, covered in lava, I scoop her into my arms and activate my Boots of Leaping. One, two, three bounds and we cross the entire floor just as the ceiling collapses. The stones land in the pools of lava, splashing the hot liquid everywhere.

By the time we reach the ground floor, the lava is already streaming from the ceiling and spreading out across the floor. We ignore the traps and charge down the middle of the room. Most of the buzz saws dangle from the ceiling, the mechanics of the traps destroyed by the lava. Some lay on the floor, the compartment that once held them gone, open to the crumbling temple above. But some are still intact. They swing for us, scraping against our backs as we rush forward.

I can see the door.

My viewpoint is turning red when another spinning blade digs into my back. I'm dying. Cyren gets hit as well. She's stumbling. Her feet aren't catching up to her momentum. The walls are falling around us. Hunks of black stone start to fall in front of the door.

We're only six feet away from the safety of the courtyard, but I know we're not going to make it.

I slam the palms of my hands into Cyren's back as the last of the temple strikes our heads. She's thrown forward, through the rock and stone and dust.

It's the last thing I see before complete blackness.

00110011

"The Temple of Ultimate Evil has killed you."

I wait, but I don't hear any other deaths. No one else in the group died, which means *she* lived. Cyren lived. That's all that matters.

There is nothing around me. In fact, there is no *me*. I'm not anywhere. There is a lack of existence, an emptiness that penetrates my form. When I thought about death, I always pictured a world of black, that I would be floating in some kind of space, but there is nothing.

"Prepare for respawn."

I haven't allowed the words to register when the game world fades into view. First large, blurry, pixelated blocks pop into the blackness. As they continue to multiply, thousands, then millions, then billions of tiny dots form graphics that are indistinguishable from reality.

I'm standing in the middle of an ancient tomb. A fire is snapping around a pile of wood. The flames allow me to see the yellowish stone of the walls. It looks like the design used in the desert zone, but I can't be sure. My message notification is beeping in the corner of my viewpoint. Cyren's voice comes from behind me. It sounds exhausted.

"It worked."

When I turn around, she's standing among a group of civilians. Each one of them has a code book open, and each one of them is holding the large quill that allows them to rewrite the code inside.

Cyren runs toward me and throws her arms around my shoulders. I hug her, but when my hands wrap around her, I touch the wounds open across her back. I step away and look at her bruised face. Her split bottom lip, red with blood. Her torn, leather-strapped outfit hangs from her body in shreds.

"You're... wounded."

I swipe my hand in the air and open my inventory. I scroll through my magic items until I find my collection of health potions.

"Here."

She hesitates, but reluctantly accepts the glowing red bottle. She pours the liquid down her throat and wipes her mouth with the back of her hand. Her wounds glow for a few seconds and disappear. Even her clothes mend themselves, the potion rejuvenating her entire avatar. She smiles, crying and laughing at the same time. She touches my face, like she's making sure it's solid.

"You're the one who died, but of course you're worried about *my* scratches."

"I died?"

I catch up all at once and I feel like I'm going to fall over, like the world is twisting on an axis that shouldn't exist. I look down at my body. I'm completely healed. A fresh avatar.

"I died! How am I... what happened? How did I respawn? How am I here?"

She clasps both of my hands inside of her own.

"A lot has happened since you died."

"Tell me," I beg, trying uselessly to contain myself.

"You were right. There were more monsters. Deeper into the zones on the other side of the Darkfyre Mountains. The battle drew them to us. They were higher Levels than we've ever seen before. We think the designers meant them for end game quests. Raids."

She closes her eyes, trying to push past the pain of the memories.

"But after you died, we were helpless. With your death, the Level Zeros had no Level. The monsters chased us back toward DangerWar City." She pauses. "Not all of us made it."

The pain is obvious, like every breath she's taking is another moment she has to live with their deaths.

"But those of us who survived, those of us who managed to run fast enough... we spread out into small groups to warn the civilians and hide them in the bonus zones, behind the secret doors. I led my group here, to the labyrinth under the desert."

"The labyrinth," I mumble. My mind is foggy and slow, like my thoughts are too thick to process. "That was smart. We cleared this place a long time ago. Monsters would never find the entrance to the hidden chambers."

She bows her head as her words whimper and fail. "Others tried to reach the secret doors in the city."

I reach out and touch her, trying to offer her as much of my strength as I can summon. "What happened to them?"

She closes her eyes tight, trying to shut off the desperate need to weep as she whispers, "It was a slaughter. The monsters... they destroyed everything. The city is..."

She pulls away from my touch and inhales, summoning her own strength to continue.

"Those of us that survived, that were able to remain hidden, we knew we had to figure out a way to end the death loop that you were in. The civilians came up with the idea to change your spawn point so that you'd reappear inside the game instead of outside the gates, in NextWorld."

I take a long, deep breath. I'm trying to allow all the pieces of the puzzle to find their place, but they keep spinning. I look down at my avatar again, studying my hands and my clothes. I feel new. Fresh. Untouched. I pull out one of my pistols. It looks shiny, like I've never fired it. I spin the cylinder of bullets.

Cyren leans in and rests her head against my chest. "I made a selfish choice. We should have let you go, let you log-out. This world... it's falling apart. It's dangerous and—"

I cup her face in my hands, look directly into her eyes, and this time I speak honestly, because there's one thing I'm sure of. "You're the reason I keep playing. You're the reason I stayed. As long as you're by my side, nothing else matters."

She shakes her head and wipes her eyes. "I don't mean to be like this. It's these emotions. I'm still trying to figure out how to handle the way I'm feeling. It's like this flood of passionate responses to everything around me."

She can sympathize and empathize and experience what's going on inside of herself and other people. She's getting in touch with emotions she doesn't recognize, because it's the first time she's ever felt them. She may have learned what it means to be human, but only on an intellectual level from whatever books were available in the game's library. Now she's experiencing it firsthand.

She's looking at me like she wants my help. She wants me to explain to her what it all means. The happiness and the sadness and the anxiety and the excitement. But the only thing I've ever felt is love.

"Arkade," she says my name as she reaches out and touches my hand. "There's something else you need to know."

"What is it?"

She glances back at the civilians, but they're focused on their code books, not our conversation. When she speaks, she's unable to look at me.

"It took them a long time to change the code. They had to be careful. Changing code is dangerous. If they made a mistake..."

I wait with a blank face, oblivious to what she's about to say. I can hear the struggle in her voice, something internal, like she's unable to speak.

"How long did it take? How long was I in the loop?"

She grabs both my hands, but she still isn't looking at me. She can't. She squeezes, letting me know she's there with me. Letting me know she's strong, so I can be weak.

"You were dead for two years."

00110100

The labyrinth is silent other than the constant scribbling of the quill pens that the civilians are using to correct the code in their books. They are still finding errors caused by the change in my spawn point.

Cyren stands next to me, her body cold and defeated. I place my arm around her, trying to comfort her, to let her know she's safe again, but her mind is elsewhere. In another time. Another place.

I know I should be more concerned with the years I've lost in my life, all the changes that have happened in my absence, but my mind keeps coming back to one thing.

"How many?" I ask.

Cyren looks at me, waiting for more.

"How many died while I was gone?"

She lowers her head, facing the fear of answering the question with a bashful hesitancy.

"Nine thousand, three hundred and eighty-seven."

I stumble backward, as if the truth shoved me away from her. My fists clench.

"The Level Zeros?"

She bites her lip, trying a different pain. "Including me, there are twenty-seven of us left."

I feel distant from the truth, like the number is so unreal that I'm unsure of its meaning. I should have been there. I vow right then to never let another NPC fall. It's a foolish, naive promise, one I know that's impossible for me to keep, yet it's all I have. It's all I can offer. The past is gone, written in code, but the future scrolls ahead of me. I have to be in control of something.

There's a tapping above us that breaks the silence.

"Rain," Cyren says when she sees my confusion.

I look up at the stonework of the ceiling. Above that are the grains of sand that cover the desert zone. Above that are the clouds in the sky that cover all of *DangerWar 2*.

I've never seen a real sky before. My dad always promised to take me on a tour of the upper levels of our tower, but we never found the time. Work and school and the growing distance between us got in the way. It doesn't matter. I doubt it's as beautiful as a virtual sky, even during a storm. In this world, everything is meticulously crafted, shaped, and reworked until every last detail is exactly what the designer pictured in their imagination. This is better than the "real world."

But the real world is still there.

I sit down on the stone bench along one wall and open my message screen. The most recent attempts to contact me are from my father. It surprises me. Even if someone within the government alerted him that I fell into the log-out loop, that I was trapped in a coma state, I can't imagine him caring. It would be no different than me being "trapped" inside the game. It changes nothing for him. In the real world I'm a body. A hunk of flesh lying in an E-Womb.

I try to push away the painful thoughts and mindlessly scroll through the endless list of message requests. I smile as I realize ninety percent of them are from Xen and Raev. Of course they are. I choose "Delete All" and select "New Connection."

It takes a few seconds before the screen opens in front of me, but instead of Xen's smiling face, the image on the screen wobbles for a second before dissolving into monochromatic static. Ones and Zeros scroll down the screen, separated by black and white pixels. I swipe at it, but my gestures aren't activating any commands.

The civilians all scream at the same time, "Turn it off!"

I keep swiping my hands at the screen, but it retracts from my grasp and explodes into a cloud of digital noise.

"What's happening?" I ask as panic tries to collapse my chest.

"The firewall is down!"

I stand up, but I don't know what to do.

"How did that happen?"

The civilians are flipping through pages, scanning each line of code at lightning fast speeds.

"The spawn point. It forced the firewall to shut down so that it could slip you back into the game."

I look over to Cyren. She appears frozen next to me, her body unable to react to the news.

"What was the firewall protecting us from?" I ask her, reaching out and touching her arm. "What else got through?"

As soon as I touch her, she jerks, catching up to the present. She leaps to her feet and rushes to the door, throwing it open and running down the halls of the underground labyrinth as fast as she can. I follow her, but by the time I catch up to her, she's outside the hidden entrance to the labyrinth, standing in the cold sand of the desert night, helplessly staring upward.

"What are you doing?" I yell over the pounding rain and howling winds. "We shouldn't be outside. The monsters could—"

The rain comes to a sudden stop. The clouds twitch, turning from a gray mist to flashing, monochromatic static.

"What is happening?" I ask.

Cyren is silent as we watch the static spread out. Black-and-white pixels flash on and off randomly, like the entire game is glitching. I glance at Cyren's face. The hyper strobe effect of the sky is bouncing off her porcelain skin. Her contemplation is stoic as she peers upward, but there's a look in her eyes that I can't quite place. It's like she's struggling against another emotion, fighting against an overwhelming feeling that's threatening to knock her over. But she remains resilient.

"Cyren. What is that?"

She turns her shaking eyes toward me. The flashing lights of the static gleam from the tears forming on the surface. When her pupils have locked onto mine, she squeezes my hand.

"It's a virus."

00110101

From high above, echoing through the world, we hear a groaning noise that sounds like an aching hunger inside the stomach of a giant. The concussive blast of the sound sends out a wave of sand and throws us both to the ground. I cover my ears, trying to stop the noise from shattering my ear drums.

When I scramble to my feet, I can see the distortion of the sky bending outward, like something is pushing on it from the other side. The pixels and the binary code elongate as the sky stretches downward. It keeps growing until it reaches its maximum tension. The groaning stops and the distorted static hangs there, teasing me with a moment of peace. I believe, for half of a second, that it's over.

Then the sky shatters.

Each tiny pixel bursts out in a radius, sprinkling to the ground like the ash of war. In its wake, it leaves a hole where there are no clouds, there are no stars, there is only the blackness, the emptiness, the nothingness that surrounded me upon my death.

That scene, that image, freezes me in place. My feet weigh twenty times more than they should. My muscles weaken. I can't move. I can't speak. I can't do anything other than stare at the hole in the world.

Cyren is yelling something from behind me, but I'm not listening. Her hand sets on my shoulder, pulling me away from the moment, but nothing inside me acknowledges her existence. I'm lost in the face of oblivion.

"Arkade!" she screams my name, her voice powerful and desperate.

It shakes me. I'm able to turn, however slowly, and see the terror in her face.

"Run!" she yells, pulling on my arm.

Her words don't make sense.

"Run? From what?"

Time slows down. Her eyes raise from me to the sky. She pulls harder.

"From that!"

I turn and look over my shoulder even as her Level 100 strength rips me from my immobile fear. My feet stumble through the sand, trying to move sideways because I can't tear my eyes away from the sky.

From the blackness, the coiled body of a giant worm descends toward the world. Its wrinkled flesh unfolds as it stretches toward the ground. Its movement seems slow, but I soon realize it appears that way because of its size. The mouth of the beast opens and a thousand razor sharp teeth encircle the gaping maw, spinning around the circumference like an inverted buzz saw. Inside the mouth is an endless throat of nothingness, waiting to swallow anything. Everything.

Cyren's hand grips my wrist tighter. She's screaming, but the words are incoherent above the heartbeat that's throbbing in my ears. My feet move faster, trying to catch up to her. She's dragging me, I know it, but I still can't look away from the apocalyptic monster plummeting toward the desert.

Right as the mouth of the worm reaches the ground, the tail breaks free from the hole in the sky, leaving the emptiness behind it. When the worm plunges into the desert floor, I'm expecting some immense quake, like a bomb that will shake the world, but there's no impact. It's as if the desert disappears as the rotating teeth devour it. The worm dives deep into the sand before curling back upward, leaving the absence of anything in its wake.

It's consuming.

Swallowing.

Deleting.

The terror in my body forces me to look away. I can't comprehend what I'm seeing. Logic is taking too long to process. I go primal. Fight or flight. I dig my boots into the sand, pushing myself away from the threat. Cyren doesn't need to drag me anymore. We're both running at full speed.

We cross over a large dune when my gamer brain kicks in. I swipe my hand in the air and open my inventory of magic items. My muscle memory helps me scroll to the exact spot in the alphabet for my Boots of Speed. I replace my Boots of Leaping in my magic item load-out, scoop up Cyren in my arms, and speed across the surface of the desert, leaving a cloud of sand in the wake of my dashing feet.

I can't help stealing a glance over my shoulder. There's a broken horizon, like an incomplete puzzle. The desert floor ends in jagged edges, revealing the obliteration of the worm's deletion. Voided areas of annihilation streak across the sky, crisscrossing trails of black left by the worm's flight through the game world. It continues, back and forth, systematically annihilating the entirety of the desert zone.

My constant push forward stretches our distance from the worm, but I don't let myself rest. When we reach the edge of the zone, I urge myself forward. My Boots of Speed burn into the pavement of the highway, toward the ruins of DangerWar City.

When the first exit sign appears, I realize I don't know where I'm going. I have no plan. I have no strategy. I yell before I know what I'm saying. I'm blubbering, my words tumbling out of my lips with a desperate speed.

"I don't know what to do! What do I do?"

"I'm contacting the remaining Level Zeros. They're collecting as many civilians as they can. We'll rendezvous with them in the city."

"The city?" I don't understand how she could be directing us toward more danger. "What about the end game monsters?"

"The Level Zeros are back at Level 100 now that you're alive again. We should be able to handle any monster if we're all together."

How is she staying so calm and collected? She's the one I'd expect to be out of control, overwhelmed with emotion. I'm supposed to be the logical one, yet here I am, shaking like I'm freezing to death.

She places her hands on my shoulders and squeezes. There's a gentleness mixed with a firm reassurance. It's calming and invigorating all at the same time. She leans in and places her mouth next to my ear again. I feel her breath as she whispers, "I love you."

I was hoping for a game plan. I was hoping for a strategy. I was hoping for a clear set of instructions that I could follow to an ultimate goal. That's what I thought I needed. But she gives me three simple words and brings my mind back to where it belongs.

I dig my feet into the pavement and head to the right, turning off the highway and running down the off-ramp. When we turn on to the street that heads toward downtown, I twist my head and look back at the desert sky. It's almost completely gone. A few chunks of cloud still remain, but otherwise there is only blackness. We're too far away to see the worm. I'm thankful for that.

After I released the players from the game, the civilians went about cleaning up all the destruction that remained after the restrictions were removed from the monsters. The world looked livable again. But now, as we reach the main street of DangerWar City, I'm able to see the destruction that happened while I was dead.

The clouds that cover the sky only add to the gray decay of the city. Beams of steel lie crooked and broken, like the skeletons of rotting corpses. No windows remain, only shattered glass. Signs for stores are no longer connected to their bases. Street lamps lie shattered across the pavement and vehicles lie overturned on the streets. The pavement is cracked from the impact of brute force, scratched by claws and talons, blackened by the scorch marks of magic and explosives. It looks like the apocalypse, but I know better. The apocalypse is still eating the desert.

I scan the skyline of demolished structures and see one building standing tall above the others, somewhat still intact. I nudge Cyren and point to it.

"We'll make our stand there."

Cyren closes her eyes and wordlessly sends a text-cast to all twenty-seven Level Zeros in our group.

As we near the high rise, I run toward the ramp that leads to the underground parking garage. As we pass the gate, I set Cyren down and we enter the darkened area slowly. I swipe my hand in the air and select a torch from my inventory. Flames burst from the end of the wooden stick. There are a few cars still parked in their spots, but the rest of the area looks empty.

I'm ready to declare the area safe when a mummy shambles out from behind a van, dirty white cloth draped around its entire body. Glowing red eyes turn toward us from between the wrappings on its head. It throws out one hand and the cloth wrapped around its arm uncoils, flying straight at us like a hissing snake. We both leap to the side and the cloth shoots past. Cyren lands in a perfect, defensive, crouched position. I roll to the side, throwing the torch to the ground and coming up with both pistols drawn.

It's nice to shoot something again. It's good to do something that I can wrap my brain around, to accomplish a clear goal that I understand. It makes sense. Point and shoot. Simple. Concise. Logical.

The cylinders of my pistols spin so fast that they sizzle, releasing automatic gunfire that streams from the barrels. The bullets tear apart the undead creature, the dried flesh ripped from its body as each round explodes. I think I'm winning, but as fast as I can decimate the enwrapped mummy, the white gauze continues to multiply, healing every hole I make.

"How strong is this thing?" I yell over my own gunfire.

The wrapping shoots out again. This time I'm not quick enough, too focused on my offense and not enough on my defense. The mummy yanks hard on the strand of cloth that snares my hand. I'm thrown from my feet. My face smashes into the concrete floor. It drags me closer so that it can land its final blow.

Cyren leaps at the creature, slamming the side of her foot into the mummy's head. It lets out a painful moan and stumbles backward. She strikes again with her palm. Her hand penetrates the dried, flaky skin of its chest and bursts out the back. She lets out an enraged scream and lifts the creature into the air, spinning it in mid air and slamming it down hard. Its arm breaks free from its body, but the cloth wrappings intertwine, pulling the limb and torso back together.

As the cloth retracts from me to heal the mummy, I scurry away from the monster, joining Cyren at a safer distance.

"We can't survive this," Cyren yells back. "They designed this for ten, maybe twenty players."

I'm ready to run away, to give up, to lose yet another battle, when I hear someone from behind us say, "Maybe *we* can help."

I turn toward the voice and see the blond barbarian stomping down the ramp into the parking garage. He's flanked by numerous Level Zeros, each one carrying a different weapon. The melee forces charge toward the mummy, while the ranged attackers unleash a storm of arrows, bullets, and rockets. In less than thirty seconds, a pile of dried, flaky remains lie on the ground where the enemy used to be. When the dust settles, the barbarian approaches me and I clasp hands with him, thanking him for his good timing.

"I'm glad you're back." He flashes me a cocky smirk. "I missed being Level 100."

I laugh, letting myself appreciate the moment of triumph, but that moment is shattered almost as soon as it appears when we hear the bellowing moan of the worm from outside the parking garage. It sounds far off, but I know it's headed this way.

And it's hungry.

00110110

"I want snipers in the corners," I say, pointing to the edges of the rooftop.

A robotic cyclops makes hand gestures to the three remaining snipers in his team. They spread out and set their high-tech rifles on tripods, adjusting their scopes and scanning the disappearing horizon.

We can all see the worm now. Its mammoth form curls over the rooftops of the city, looking as if it's inhaling existence itself. It leaves behind an imposing trail of deletion, blackness that exists in the absence of the world. I wonder what will happen even if we *can* stop it. Will we move on, accepting this new edge to our reality, a cliff into the abyss that will hover over the southern horizon?

I shake the pointless worrying from my head when Cyren emerges from the stairwell.

"The civilians are fortifying the parking garage," she says before looking into the distance toward the doom that draws closer, "though I'm not sure how much good a few parked cars blocking the entrance will do."

"It's only there to stop any monsters that might wander nearby," I say, trying to keep my mind in strategy-mode. "The last thing we need to worry about are multiple opponents. I want all our attention focused on... *that*."

"I helped them gather more vehicles from the surrounding blocks," she says. "Fast ones. Just in case..."

"Smart."

I hate considering failure, but we need to have an escape plan, even if I have no idea where we could run.

"I don't understand where that thing came from. Who would want to attack this game with a virus?"

I stop to consider her question, then shake my head and say, "There will be time to worry about that later." I hope. "We need to focus."

The group of Level Zeros silently prepare themselves. A part of me wishes they hadn't spent so much time studying and developing their emotional depth. Maybe then they wouldn't know fear. What I see in their eyes, I have to assume, is the dread of what awaits them.

For them, deletion is death.

The worm reaches the edge of the city, and we all watch in horror as it destroys the first of the buildings. The beast shaves off the top ten floors in one swoop, turning into the park and scooping out the ground as it swings around to obliterate the rest of the building. It coils and retracts, its flabby bulk sagging and bulging as it consumes the contents of our world. Its movements seem random, but I continue to watch, counting out the seconds before each twist, each turn, each dive, and each reemergence from below. Within a few minutes, a pattern appears.

"Listen up!" I yell, calling out to the entire group.

My words are so fast and excited that I need to consciously slow myself down. My hands slash through the air, physically describing the pattern. The Level Zeros nod their heads. This is math. This is logic. There's no need to explain a second time.

"The snipers are going to have the greatest distance with their attacks, so they're going to fire first. We don't know if that will draw its attention, but even if its direction changes, it will most likely fall right back into the same pattern. Watch for the signals, the twitches. You'll be able to predict what it's going to do, and that will give us the advantage."

I point at the two remaining Level Zeros left in the demolitions team. "You're up next. We want a huge volley as soon as that thing comes within range. Look for weak spots and concentrate your fire there. Normally I'd say to aim for the mouth, but that thing is a vacuum. It would delete your explosives like everything else. We need to destroy the body."

I motion toward the leader of the ranged team, a woman in a bright red suit and fedora carrying an ancient Thompson submachine gun. "Then it's your turn. If that thing comes anywhere near us, I want a wave of bullets crashing against its body every second that it's within range."

She and her team take position.

Turning around to talk to Cyren, I notice her stance is stiff, with her hands clasped behind her back. She's in full-on soldier mode, ready to take my commands with a salute of confidence. She stands in front of her melee team, all fifteen of them mimicking her exact posture. They're the biggest group, with the most survivors, all of them armed with swords, clubs, and spears. I understand her need to be professional in front of her troops, so I resist the urge to offer her comfort.

"You have the most important role." I'm speaking to Cyren, but loud enough so the whole team can hear me. "It's also the most dangerous."

I point at the worm spiraling into the sky, deleting a large gray cloud that hangs over what used to be the city park.

"It's going to require some precise timing, but when that things comes near us, I want you to jump on top of it."

The eyes of the team grow large, but Cyren doesn't flinch. She accepts my words without hesitation. Her strength emanates outward and the rest of the team finds their bravery in her, settling back into a firm, defiant stance.

"Use everything you've got," I say. "Carve into that thing. Open up wounds that our sniper and demolitions teams can exploit."

"Yes, sir!" the entire team shouts with a salute.

When they spread out to take their positions, Cyren lingers. Her face softens. She reaches out and wraps her fingers around my arm, squeezing a bit.

"It's a good plan."

I let out a breath. "It's *a* plan. We'll find out how good it is if we survive."

"We couldn't do this without you."

"I know. You need my Level to—"

"No," she says with a sharp yet quiet voice. "We need *you*. You're an amazing player. You can look at this game like no one else does. Not even us." She gives me a knowing smile. "And they programmed us to play."

"Sometimes I think I was too." I look out over the world, watching the worm delete everything I've held dear to me. "All that time, in all those games... I always felt what I was doing was important. More important than I could explain to anyone else. It was like every shot, every kill, every skill I learned... it was all building up to something."

"Maybe it was."

"Maybe," I say.

She grabs my face, her leather gloves holding on to my cheeks, forcing me to look into her eyes.

"No matter what happens today, no matter how this turns out, whether we win or lose, you must know how cherished you are in this world. You've already sacrificed more for us than any other player ever has."

I do my best impersonation of someone confidently accepting her words, but when I turn away from her and look out over the city, only to see the worm dive from the sky and devour half of a shopping mall, I can't help wondering how many more sacrifices I'll be making.

00110111

The robotic cyclops counts down for his sniper team, timing their first shots all at once. The rest of us stand with our weapons gripped tightly in our hands. I tap my foot as each second counts off. When the cyclops reaches zero, and the four sniper rifles fire in unison, it makes me jump. I'm not startled by the noise. It's the simple release of anticipation, the thrust into the present. I can't think about "what ifs" anymore. It's happening right now. I need to stay ahead of the game.

The bullets strike the thick skin of the worm, but they leave no trace of damage. The worm continues on its path, carving into an already bombed-out office building twenty blocks away. Its gargantuan body digs into the ground, leaving a pit of nothingness where the street used to be, before turning back up as its programming tells it to.

"Again!" I shout.

The sniper team fires. Still nothing.

It doesn't exactly inspire anyone. Is this thing following the same rules that we are? Can it take damage? Am I misreading it because of its graphical representation? I ignore my doubts. We have a plan. We have to stick to it.

"Keep firing!" I turn to the rest of the group and yell over the gunfire, "If it doesn't change its movements, at least we'll know when it's coming for us."

It doesn't take long. The worm devours entire city blocks in just a few swoops. As it destroys a nearby complex of buildings, the demolitions team steps up. Rockets stream across the sky and explode in blooming clouds of fire as they strike the worm. We all wait with anticipation as the smoke clears. There is an unspoken reaction of disappointment that washes over us when we see the worm descend toward the street without a single mark.

The sniper team continues to fire. The demolitions team releases six more volleys of rockets before the head of the worm makes its preprogrammed turn toward our building. All six members of the ranged team raise their weapons as the melee team readies themselves to launch into the air.

Our group's barrage blocks my view. It's a constant rattle of gunfire all around me. The Level 100 attacks of bullets and rockets and explosions turn the sky into a blinding storm of warfare. When my eyes adjust to the chaos, I see the worm break through, pushing past the rolling fire and the swarm of explosive rounds. It falls toward the building slowly, and I'm able to gauge the true size and magnitude of the creature. Its shadow casts over us like an approaching storm. I can see behind the spinning rows of teeth, directly into the blackness, the void widening as it draws closer.

My hope is lost.

Luckily, my feet know what to do. I run to the side of the rooftop with the melee team as my gamer instincts calculate the worm's descent. I watch the worm crash into the rooftop, shaving off half of the building as it drops. The teeth continue to spin inside the mouth, helping the creature inhale the graphics like they are simply breaths of air.

As the worm falls, the underside of its belly rolls past. Among the flabby mounds of flesh, I notice a symbol marked on its skin. It falls past me so fast that I barely have time to see a single logo that looks like two question marks, back to back, before it drifts out of view.

The melee team rushes past me, toward the massive body. Reaching the edge of the rooftop, they leap into the air, latching on to folds of flesh as the beast rumbles past. They drop from view, carried on the worm's back like parasites. When the tail drops below the building, I follow the ranged team as they rush to the fractured edge.

It's a strange thing, staring down into nothing. There is no sense of depth. No height to judge how far up we are. In the dimensionless field of black, the tail of the worm grows smaller until it swoops back around for another pass.

The tiny bodies attached to the side use their weapons to pound and slash and stab at the flesh, trying to break through, but they aren't making any progress.

The worm chews through the neighboring office building, deleting a diagonal slash through the structure. Two of the melee team are scraped off the side as the worm slides past the steel and concrete walls. Their limbs flail as they tumble into the black, disappearing in to the emptiness.

The leader of the ranged team, the woman with the red suit and fedora, stops firing her Tommy gun and leans in closer to me, shouting, "This isn't working!"

I grit my teeth. I try to summon the puzzle in my brain. My problem-solving abilities rise up, ready to tackle the question in front of me, but nothing happens. I hit a wall. There is no solution. The invincible worm will continue its relentless deletion until there is nothing left.

I can't kill that which will not die.

I can't escape when there is nowhere left to go.

Deep within my stomach, there's a boiling, festering frustration that burns me from the inside. I want to lash out. I want to stomp my feet and yell at the game.

"This isn't fair!"

There are supposed to be rules. There are supposed to be laws and limitations. There are supposed to be balanced powers that give everyone an equal chance. This isn't a game. I can't win.

So I decide to cheat.

"Fall back!"

I send the group-wide audio-cast and back up toward the stairs. As the worm dives at our building, the melee team leaps from its back. The remaining twelve Level Zeros land with precision on the rooftop and join the rest of the group running toward me. I hold the door open for them, and when Cyren runs in last, I spin through the opening and follow the group down.

We're racing as fast as we can, leaping four or five stairs at a time, using the railing to keep our balance. Not being able to see the worm from inside means we can no longer calculate its approach. I try to mentally picture it in my head, but by the time we've descended ten floors, I've lost track of my orientation.

We descend another five or six floors before I hear the hollow moaning of the worm outside the building. Directly below me, the beast cuts the building in half, deleting floors thirty-five through fifty-one. What remains of the top half of the building still floats in the air as if the deleted section was still holding it up. Past the blackness, three Level Zeros look back at me in horror from the lower floors. I stand with Cyren and two others, the rest of the group swallowed. Gone. Their existence erased.

Cyren's fists clench. The other two Level Zeros look at me with a panicked sadness, but we don't have time to mourn. We don't have time to remember our fallen comrades. We need to survive.

"Grab on to me," I shout, holding out my arms.

There's a moment of confusion, but I thrust my hands toward them. They fumble, but eventually find a tight grip on my trench coat. I step off the deleted staircase and activate my Anti-Gravity Belt. The weight of all four of us still pulls us through the black at an accelerated rate, but the belt gives us enough pause to tumble on to the staircase below unharmed. We waste no more time and run down the rest of the stairs as fast as we can. I hear the worm pass overhead a few more times, devouring the rest of the rooftop and the remaining upper floors.

When we erupt from the doorway into the underground parking lot, half of the area is gone. A row of cars and trucks idle near the gate, packed full of civilians, but not as many as there were before. I can see a look on their faces that must be mourning. It deepens when they see only seven of us running toward them.

I don't have time to explain anything. I swing myself into the bed of a pickup truck and Cyren joins me. As soon as the other Level Zeros find a vehicle I shout, "Move!"

The tires squeal as each vehicle launches up the ramp, turning on to what remains of the street. I tell them to head east, toward the ocean, while I watch the worm continue its ruthless decimation of the city behind us. I can't look away, but when I hear Cyren say my name, I pull my gaze forward. The group in the back of the truck are all staring at me, all awaiting some kind of order. Some kind of direction. They want a plan.

I look into Cyren's eyes and among the sparkles of light that reflect back toward me, I see her. The real her. The girl I love. I realize, in that moment, that I'm no longer playing a game. I'm only fighting to win another day with her. So I push past my disdain for cheating and I accept the absence of rules.

"I need you to change the code," I yell to the civilian dressed like a baker that is sitting near the back of the truck.

"What can we do?" The baker summons his code book and opens it up, flipping through the pages, showing me how many are now blank. "That worm isn't a part of the game. It doesn't exist in the code."

"But the airport does," I say as I look forward, toward the untouched coastline.

"The airport?" Cyren asks, flashing a nervous look over her shoulder at the rest of the group. "Escaping in a plane would only be a temporary solution. Eventually we'll run out of fuel."

"I know." I flash a smile of confidence at the baker and say, "That's what I need you to change."

00111000

While our caravan of vehicles makes its way out of the city and travels down the coastline, toward the airport, I'm still watching the worm. I'm timing its consumption against our speed and I don't like our odds.

"How's it coming?"

As the baker searches the text that scrolls across the page of his code book, he holds up one finger, as if to silence me.

Cyren tries to assure me by saying, "I have faith they can accomplish a simple hack of an airplane's fuel supply. They were able to change your spawn point—"

"When they changed my spawn point, they brought down the game's firewall and let in a virus."

She cracks her knuckles. "Fair enough."

"At this point, I'm not worried about if they can do it or not," I say, looking away from her at the great beast consuming the sky. "I'm worried about how *fast* they can do it."

"With their combined processing power, it shouldn't be long."

"I hope you're right. I just—"

The driver of our truck locks his brakes and I'm thrown against the cab. Peering over the top of the cab, I see two Level Zeros climbing out of a van that's now parked sideways on the street.

They lift their guns and raise their barrels upward. I follow their aim, instinctively pulling my own pistols from their holsters, readying myself for whatever flying monster is approaching. But the threat isn't in the sky, it's towering over us.

Two Tyrannosauruses are charging down the middle of the road, their mouths hanging open, salivating at the sight of us. Their powerful hind legs crack the pavement with every lunging step they take toward us.

The Level Zeros ahead of me start firing and Cyren is already leaping over the side of the truck, ready to join the battle by the time I register what's happening. I'm trying to keep too many things balanced in my head. The multitasking is slowing down my reaction time. I glance over my shoulder at the worm, calculate its approximate distance, and then turn back toward the immediate threat.

As the bullets pierce the first dinosaur's hide, trails of blood stream behind it. I let out a sigh of relief. Finally something that we can hurt. My own pistols join the gunfire, tearing small chunks from its body. A Level Zero lets loose a rocket, which slams squarely into one monster's chest. The attack on the first dinosaur is continuous, draining the creature's hit points until it falls face first into the street. Its body lays motionless as the second one climbs over it.

When the remaining dinosaur reaches the lead car in our caravan, it lowers its head, sinks its teeth into the station wagon, and scoops it up from the street. The back door opens up and civilians fall out, like dolls falling to the pavement. They crash into the street, some of them able to get up and run, while others roll around in agony.

The dinosaur shakes its head, whipping the vehicle back and forth. When it opens its mouth, the empty car is flung toward our group. The vehicle crashes into the street, rolling end over end, scattering everyone. I leap to the side as the car crashes into the pickup truck next to us. The collision crushes two more civilians as I roll off the side of the road and watch the dinosaur devour the crippled civilians near its feet.

I should be sad, or at least reacting to the constant string of deaths, but all I can think about is the time we're wasting. This is taking too long, and now we're down two vehicles. Right now I'm looking at things on such a macro level that the details of individual deaths are insignificant compared to a giant virus that is eating the world.

I'm about to order everyone to focus their gunfire on the dinosaur's face, hoping to score critical hits and increase our damage output, but Cyren is one step ahead of me.

As she leaps toward the dinosaur, it sees her coming and opens its mouth, ready to snatch its next snack right out of the air. Cyren contracts her body at the last second and slides past the giant teeth, and as soon as she's inside the creature's mouth, she lashes out with all of her limbs. Her feet stamp down on the dinosaur's tongue and the palms of her hands slam against the roof of its mouth. Her muscles struggle for a few more seconds as the dinosaur's jaws try to squeeze shut, but her Level 100 strength wins the fight. With a sickening snap of bones, the jaw breaks, falling open and dangling loosely as the creature roars in pain. Cyren jumps to safety as the remaining Level Zeros and I unleash another hail of gunfire. The helpless monster twists and turns as each round explodes, finally toppling on to the street.

There is a strange moment of silence as we all brush ourselves off and look around in stunned astonishment at the devastation these two monsters caused. The bellowing moan of the approaching worm snaps me back into my panicked momentum.

"Let's get moving!" I yell, shouting out commands to the group, telling them which vehicle they should get into to spread the Level Zeros out among the surviving civilians.

I climb into the back of a van as it lurches forward, building speed as the worm devours the last of the city behind us. The civilians return to their task, opening their code books and searching for an answer to our fuel problem.

We travel down the coastline and reach the airport in under three minutes. Other than the wreckage of a few jets out on the tarmac, the place looks abandoned. I'm worried that we might not find a working plane, but when the lead vehicle crashes through the chain-link fence, I see a cargo jet that looks untouched on the runway.

I point us toward the airplane and watch the worm make its way up the coast, consuming the beaches and harbors that line the city. It's drawing closer. I know we don't have much time.

We park behind the plane and the civilians race up the open ramp, buckling themselves into seats that line the walls of the aircraft. As soon as they're strapped in, they open their code books and return to their search. Two Level Zeros run toward the cabin to start the preparations for takeoff. I take position with the other four near the rear of the plane in case there are any other monsters inhabiting the airport. I'm not going to let anything else delay us.

No one speaks. We watch in silence as the worm skims the coastline, deleting everything on its way toward us. I hold on to one of my pistols, foolishly allowing it to give me some sense of comfort, even though I know it's pointless. There's nothing we can do against the virus. Nothing. Our only hope is to run.

As the mouth of the worm crashes into the side of the airport, it shaves off the tower that rises above the terminal and the body of the immense creature sinks below the ground.

I look at Cyren. She looks back at me and a smile lifts the corners of her black lips. It's weak, but I know it's taking every ounce of her strength to offer it to me.

"Arkade? I want you to know..."

"What is it?"

"It's okay if we fail."

"We're not going to fail."

She reaches out and grabs my hand.

"Listen to me. I want you to know that if this is the end, if we never see each other ever again, it's okay. I'm happy. I'm happy because I got to know you. I'm happy because I got to love you."

The worm rises up from the runway a few yards behind us, its mouth letting loose a moan that shakes the pit of my stomach. I calculate its trajectory and I know when it turns back toward the ground, it will consume the plane.

I yell toward the cabin door, "We need to go!"

When I don't hear a response, I move my foot forward, ready to grab Cyren's hand and run. It's a useless gesture of course, there's no way we could make it to a vehicle in time, but my heart doesn't care. I can't give up. I need to do anything I can to fight for our survival.

The sound of the jets stop me. The aircraft rolls forward as the worm turns its head, twisting its body for its descent. The plane picks up speed. The worm drops toward us. The nose of the aircraft lifts from the ground. The spinning teeth of the worm skim the tail of the plane, missing us by inches before it plunges into the ground, mindlessly unaware of our existence as it erases more of the world.

I holster my pistol and grip on to the strap above me with both hands as the rear wheels lift off the ground. Before I manage to press the button to close the rear ramp of the plane, the wind rushes past me and my cowboy hat flies from my head. It flops through the streams of air currents caused by the jets, falling toward the deleted blackness, shrinking in size as we ascend into the clouds, eventually disappearing like everything else.

00111001

From the window of the cargo jet, we watch the virus destroy our world. The sea is gone. The horizon is black. The worm annihilates the jungle acre by acre. It carves open the Darkfyre Mountains, scooping out every boulder and cliff and snow-capped peak until there is nothing left. Finally it erases the sun itself. We fly away from the mouth of the beast into the endless nothing.

There is no up or down or sense of direction. There is only us and the worm, and we aim our jet away from the mouth that is always approaching. It hunts us now, moving in a straight line, sensing the last bits of information that it must destroy.

I can't stop thinking about all that we've lost. The streets of DangerWar City that I loved. The equipment shops where I filled my inventory. The penthouse apartment where Cyren and I watched so many sunsets.

I think about Deathsand Desert. It used to be home to the doorway which at one point was my only means of escape. It's strange to think about now, after risking so much to stay, that at one point I was willing to risk so much to leave. I think about the friends that accompanied me on that journey. It felt like we could have accomplished anything. I wish they were with me now. Maybe things would have turned out differently.

I consider opening a video-cast with Xen, but when I think about the risk of unleashing yet another worm right here, inside the cargo jet, I shut the menu screen with a quick swipe of my hand.

I drop my head and close my eyes, shutting out the view of the worm's gaping maw. There is a moment of loneliness. The weight of the situation rests upon my shoulders, as if it's up to me to turn this hopeless situation around. It's my own stubbornness that fuels that fire. No one else is pressuring me to save them. In fact, there is a melancholy attitude reverberating inside the jet that isn't allowing the civilians or the Level Zeros to see a future.

But the game isn't over yet.

I barely notice Cyren sit down, her stealthy movements allowing her to slide in next to me like a breeze rather than a body. I shudder when she sets her hand atop mine. I open my eyes and meet her gaze. I can't read her state of mind, but I know she's reading mine.

"You're going to be okay," she says.

"We're all going to be okay. The civilians will change the code, hack the fuel supply, and we'll have as much time as we need to figure out a new plan."

She smiles, but I notice something different in her eyes. Is that sympathy?

Her smile doesn't break as she says, "The world is gone."

I shake my head, not wanting to hear what she's saying. "You're still here. That's all that matters. We still have the jet and—"

"Then what?"

"Then... I don't know," I say, exhausted. "At least we're still alive."

She rests her head on my shoulder and says, "This isn't living."

I reject it. I reject her. I stand up, maybe a little too forcefully, pushing her away as I do.

My voice strains defensively as I say, "That's exactly what this is. We survived. I got us away from..." I point out the window at the open mouth of the worm with its spinning teeth and hollow throat. "...*that*."

"I know that. Everyone does. You were great. You were wonderful. As always. You did as much and even more than anyone could have done."

"So what then? Is that not enough?"

She doesn't look away. She keeps gazing into me, like she's trying to cradle me with her eyes.

"You tell me."

I look around the jet. The civilians are flipping through pages, scrolling through lines of code and scribbling with their quill pens to change if/then statements and recalculate algorithms. They're working at a furious pace, but they wear a blank expression, like they're struggling to accept some kind of inevitability that only they are aware of.

The remaining Level Zeros sit in their own chairs, fiddling with their weapons, unsure of what to do now that they have nothing left to fight.

There are a few cargo containers buckled to the floor, most likely empty, only there as environmental decoration for the game. Some radar equipment sits behind a fenced off area with blinking lights and flashing screens twinkling in the corner, detecting nothing. The rest of the jet is industrial beams and bare walls. Function over form. It might not be pretty, but it's keeping us safe. It's keeping *her* safe.

"Yes," I blurt out. Confidently. Defiantly. "This *is* enough. *You* are enough. All I need is you."

She smiles again in that sympathetic way. For some reason it feels condescending, like she understands something that I don't, and she's patiently waiting for me to catch up.

"That's sweet. It really is. And I have no doubt, that at this moment in time, you believe that." The smile falters. It shakes a bit as she struggles to maintain it, and then falls away. "But I could never ask you to do that. I could never ask you to live like this."

"You don't have to. I'm making the choice on my own. This isn't a sacrifice. I get to keep living with you, and I—"

"This isn't like before. This isn't like when you chose our world over NextWorld. You'd go mad here." She looks around at the other civilians, still pouring over their code books. "We all would."

"That's not true. You'd still be able to study, and learn, and—"

She reaches out and grabs my hand. The leather glove is cold. She pulls me closer so that I'm sitting down next to her again. She puts both her arms around me and hugs me. It's forceful, but oddly comforting, like she's pressing her calm into me.

I try to push her away again, ready to argue more, but she holds on to me, her fingers gripping my trench coat and holding me in place.

"Not all of us have to die. If you log-out—"

"No!" I shout, but my lips are pressed into her shoulder. My mind flips into problem-solving mode. "We can fix the firewall. We can keep flying." I jump from idea to idea before I shake my head and say, "We'll figure something out. I'm never going to leave you. That's never been an option for me. I won't—"

"Shh," she whispers. "Sit with me for a while."

I close my eyes and do as she asks. It's actually easier than I expected to not think about anything. I inhale the smell of her leather-strapped suit and relax into her powerful arms. I feel like a child again. Something that hasn't happened in a long, long time. Since my mother.

I'm not sure how much time has passed when we hear a calm, sedated voice say, "Excuse me."

An old man wearing a tweed jacket steps next to us. He adjusts his glasses and speaks to Cyren. "We wanted to inform you that we've succeeded in changing the code."

He doesn't wait for a response. He pivots on one foot and returns to his seat. The civilians all close their code books, which disappear into their inventory and stare straight ahead. Their faces are devoid of any humanity. It's unnerving.

"That's... that's good," I say, but when I look at Cyren, she looks far from happy. I put my hand on her shoulder and say, "Cyren, I know you don't believe me, but now that we don't have to worry about fuel, we can—"

"Arkade," she says my name in a whisper and takes a deep breath before she continues. "That isn't the code that they changed."

Her words confuse me, but the ominous tone she uses causes my stomach to sink.

"What are you talking about?"

I look around the interior of the jet at all the faces of the civilians, hoping for some kind of explanation, but their eyes are vacant.

Cyren touches the side of my face and turns my gaze back toward her. Her eyes are glossy with tears, but she's holding them back, doing everything she can to stop them from falling. She stares at me for a long time. Too long.

"I knew you'd never leave me. I knew that was never an option for you." She smiles as a tear rolls down her face. "Sometimes I think I know you better than you know yourself."

She's not answering my question, and the panic inside my chest is rising from the unknown.

"What did they change?"

Her answer is simple and soft, like she's offering me a goodnight kiss.

"They changed your spawn point."

I stumble backward, away from her.

"No," I say, but no matter how strongly I mean it, it falls powerlessly from my mouth.

"It's the only chance you have. You can go on living, without fear."

"I don't want this," I say, my voice breaking with desperation. "I need to be here with you. I need to protect you. I need to save you."

She steps toward me and places her hands on either side of my head. She leans in and her kiss lingers against my lips. I lose myself, unable to focus on my own distress. She pulls away and her mouth rounds my cheek, settling in next to my ear.

She whispers, "It's time for *me* to save *you*."

She steps back from me. Her fists clench. The muscles in her arms tighten, bulging with her Level 100 strength. I want to beg her to stop and think about what she's about to do. I want to plead my case and give her a thousand reasons why I should stay. I want to step away from her, but I can't move. Seeing her as a threat is something I don't understand. My brain stalls. The moment hangs between us. She steps forward and my body shudders. I flinch, ready for her attack, but her body slackens. Her muscles relax and her fists unclench. She covers her face and begins to cry.

"I can't do it."

I let out a breath. My body melts back into the reality I know. Cyren would never hurt me. I was foolish to think she would.

"It's okay," I say, reaching out toward her. "There's no need to—"

From behind me, hands slap down on each of my shoulders, fingers digging into me. They yank me backward and I slam onto the floor of the cargo area. I'm stunned as I look up and see the faces of the remaining Level Zeros pinning me to the floor.

I hear Cyren in the distance whimpering, "I'm sorry. This is the only way to make sure you'll be okay."

I struggle, but there are too many of them. They point rifles and shotguns at me, the barrels inches from my face.

The last thing I hear is Cyren's voice.

"I love you."

My death is instantaneous.

00111010

The announcer's voice is loud and clear. It lists the names of the Level Zeros that killed me. It tells me I'm dead, but my ears deny the truth as much as my mind and my heart.

Pixels appear in the black, fading into view, multiplying their resolution. As they form, a part of me still believes that I'll see the game world of *DangerWar 2*. Maybe I'll be floating in the blackness of the deleted desert, or maybe I'll return to the inside of the cargo plane. My hopefulness would accept either, but as the world takes shape, I recognize my surroundings all too well.

DOTfun.

I'm standing outside the gates of the original *DangerWar*. Gamers of all ages are shouting and laughing, showing off the new inventory they acquired or bragging about their high score. A myriad of transports roll up, gallop up, or fly up to the gate, and players disembark, ready to start a new game session. The sky is an unrealistic shade of blue and the clouds are as white as I remember.

My eyes flash to the wall, next to the gate, where the wooden door once stood as an entrance to *DangerWar 2*, but there is nothing there. I fall to my knees. My mind is weak. Useless.

My player stats are public and available for all to see, but it takes a few seconds before one of the players notices my name in the NextWorld social system. An avatar designed to look like a skeleton stops in his tracks and points at me.

"Arkade?" he says, his voice sounding young and prepubescent. "Hey! That's the Game Master!"

A few more players stop and take notice. Some of them mumbling, which grows into arguing, which turns into shouting.

"That's not Arkade."

"Yes it is! Look at his player stats!"

"It's a hack. Someone is goofing off."

"No, she's right. Look at how much time he has logged on *DangerWar 2*."

"How did he get out?"

"What's wrong with him?"

The arguing and shouting of the growing mob is silenced when the sky above me flashes with a pulsating red light. I remain on my knees. None of this matters. I'm not here. I can't be.

"It's the DgS!"

DOTgov Security officers teleport into the domain and surround me. Their sleek, silver bodies appear androgynous and they are impossible to tell apart aside from the numbers on their backs. The officers swipe their hands in the air, raising screens full of sensors and readouts. Information scrolls past their vision. A few of them nod in agreement before one of the officers steps closer.

"User name: Arkade. We have flagged your account and will log you out immediately to be processed IRL."

I never thought I'd have to hear that acronym ever again. In Real Life. I can't process the fear that idea causes in me. It's cracking my mind in a thousand places. I'm not ready. I want to cry out, to beg them to stop, to give me one more chance. Please, please, please let me back in. But they don't give me the chance.

The officer reaches out and touches me with a hand that glows red for a second before the world collapses in on itself, shrinking to a tiny white dot in the center of my vision. The dot fades and I hear the voice that was once so common place, but now is more like a forgotten bit of nostalgia.

"Wireless connection disengaged from your nanomachines."

Tubes retract from my orifices. The long one pulling out from below my waist is uncomfortable enough, but I choke when the feeding tube pulls itself from my throat.

"Biological connections disengaged."

It's cold. No, maybe it's warm. I don't understand what my skin is telling me because I haven't felt a real temperature in years. The sensation is strange and it takes a few seconds for me to adjust.

My curiosity is begging me to look around, but I keep my eyes shut. I don't want to see. Not really. Not with my actual, biological eyes. I don't want to see the dirt and the grime and the filth of the real world. I think that maybe if I keep them closed I'll fall asleep. At least I can dream. If that's as close as I can get to removing myself from this physical world, I'll take it.

"Welcome back."

I recognize the voice, but after it speaks, my brain can't locate the memory it's searching for. My eyes blink open. The brightness of the E-womb's interior light is blinding, but as my vision adjusts, I'm able to make out a blurry figure. Like the pixels in the game, my vision defines until I can see the details of the face peering through the open hatch. My brain floods with memories as the connection to the voice is made.

I see the face of my father.

00111011

My father thinks he's helping me out of the E-womb because I'm having problems moving my body after being logged-in for so long. The truth is, I don't want to move. I have an apathy for everything that's making my body refuse to cooperate.

He sets me down on the bed and I'm able to take in my surroundings. I know I'm in my old tower room. Same rust spot on the wall. Same scratches on the floor. But some things have also changed.

First of all, my E-womb has been upgraded beyond anything I could afford. It's capable of sustaining someone's life while they're logged-in to NextWorld without them ever leaving for food or digestion. It takes care of everything for you. Only the richest people can afford those. I'd be lying if I said I wasn't impressed by it.

The rest of the room is bare. The mattress on my bed has no covers. No sheets. No pillow. My body shivers in acknowledgment of the temperature.

"Sorry," my father says, waking the mirrored screen above the sink from its sleep-mode. "When you fell into the coma and your brain activity stopped, I had to convince DOTgov to continue the game world. They agreed, but they made me pay for your tower room and your E-Womb connection out of my own pocket. In order to save credits, I haven't been keeping the temperature turned up in here. Not much of a need, considering..."

He pushes a few onscreen buttons and raises a small red bar. Heat blows up from the metal-grated floor. It makes my skin ache and the smell of it reminds me of when I'd leave an old vitapaste container out too long. I push myself back on the mattress until I'm pressed against the corner of the room. It's as far away from reality as I can get.

My father sits down on the bed and says, "I knew you'd come back. I knew you'd find a way. I never gave up hope that you'd escape."

When I don't respond, he leans in close, studying my eyes as if he's searching for something. His face is flabby with wrinkles, like the flesh of the worm virus. Tough and impenetrable. It reminds me how rough his hands felt as a child, like the outside world had punished him when he was young. He puts his hand on my head and turns me back and forth so he can examine me. I can smell his breath. I squint my eyes and pull away from him.

He lets out a sigh and runs his tongue along his gums. It's an annoying habit of his. He was born with teeth and he says he never got used to them being gone. My nanomachines prevented the growth of teeth because they deemed them pointless when all I was going to eat was vitapaste. I can't imagine how weird it must have been for people to have bones in their mouths.

"I'm sure it's going to take you a bit to adjust. You were logged-in for an unhealthy amount of time."

He's worried about me being in *there*? It's *this* place that's unhealthy.

"It's funny," he says as he lets out a small laugh, turning away from me and sitting on the edge of the mattress. "I've thought a lot about what I'd say to you. Every time I tried to connect a text-cast, or an audio-cast, or a video-cast with you... I'd practice in my mind what I was going to say. I felt so prepared, like when I give a speech. Every word is carefully chosen so that no one will misconstrue anything I say. That's my job. I'm good at that. I'm good at speeches."

He leans forward, resting his elbows on his knees. He intertwines his fingers and rubs his thumbs against each other, like he's waiting for one of them to win the struggle. When he looks over his shoulder at me, our eyes catch for a split second before I look back at the bare mattress.

"But it wasn't a speech I was giving, was it? It should have been a conversation. I know that now. I should have been listening. I have all these questions for you, but I'm no good at that. I'm no good at facing the unknown. Without some kind of plan, everything is... it's just too dangerous. There's too many variables that I can't prepare for."

He looks away from me, back at his thumbs. There's a long moment of silence. I want it to end, but I don't want the conversation to continue either. I want him to leave. I want to be alone so I can be as sad as I need to be. So I can be as sad as I am.

"I've been doing my best. Your life, your upbringing, it was completely different from mine. I didn't know how to make it work. All that stuff came so naturally to your mother. I let her handle it. When she... after she was gone, I was at a loss. I tried, but everything was moving so fast, I don't think I ever had a chance to catch up."

He reaches over and sets his hand on my ankle. I pull my knees close to my chest, away from him.

"Maybe now that we have time to talk, I'll be able to explain myself. And if you can't forgive me for the mistakes I've made... maybe someday you'll at least be able to understand where I'm coming from. This is a miracle. Truly. Whatever it was that freed you from that game, it happened for a reason. And I'm not going take it for granted."

He shakes his head and lets out a groan.

"Listen to me. I'm babbling. Like I said, if I don't have a script to read, this is what happens."

He stands up from the mattress and claps his hands together. "I should let you rest. Get some actual, honest-to-goodness sleep. We can talk more later."

He walks toward the door, still talking.

"DOTgov will want to expedite your trial, for the media's sake. There's been a lot of attention to your story from parent groups since you fell into the coma. I'm guessing we'll only have a few days for me to call in some favors, but hopefully I still have some pull around the office." The door slides open and he steps out, turning to look at me one last time. "Don't worry, son. Now that I have you back, there's no way that I'm going to let you go again."

00111100

With my father gone, I manage to push myself off the mattress and drag my feet across the metal grate of the floor as fast as I can, toward the E-womb. Maybe it's denial, I don't know, but I refuse to believe I'm trapped here. I keep telling myself this is a momentary prison.

I open the hatch, crawl inside the doorway, and say, "Log-in," waiting for the lights to turn on. But they don't. The E-Womb coldly replies, "Access denied."

"No!" I spit out the word and bang my fist on the interior of the sphere. "You piece of junk! Log-in!"

"Access denied."

I groan and crawl out, banging my head on the top of the doorway as I exit. It stings, adding to my frustration. I tap my finger on the mirrored screen above the sink, hoping to contact Xen and talk to someone who understands, but the screen flashes the word LOCKED.

All I can see is my reflection. The bony figure of a young man I don't recognize. It would be easy to blame it on my age. I'm still skinny, but I'm taller. I must have grown four inches in the past three years. I actually need to bend down to see the top of my bald head in the mirror. There are the beginnings of wrinkles around my eyes and near my nose. Those weren't there before. But it isn't the age of my body that looks so unrecognizable. It's the fact that I'm no longer an avatar.

This body isn't me. I don't look like I'm supposed to look. I don't move like I'm supposed to move. It's more difficult to lift my arm. It's slower. The idea of doing a back flip or rolling across the floor sounds painful.

How does anyone live like this?

I return to the mattress and lie down. As I stare at the ceiling, I notice how loud the room is for being so empty. I can hear the hum of the machines that keep the life-support systems running. The temperature controls rattle below the floor. The air filters hiss in the walls. The entire room is vibrating. Even if I turned off the lights, the sound would deny me the escape inward that I crave. It keeps my consciousness right here, trapped in the real world.

I try to summon my own game world inside my imagination, one where Cyren and I are still together. I can see her, when I try hard enough, but it isn't real. It isn't even virtual. There are no details, nothing tangible. It's a foggy, fading memory, an undefined form that represents her but can't come close to embodying everything that she was. I remember the coldness of her leather suit, the sharp edges of every buckle. I remember every curve of her lips. I remember how her nose perked up at the tip. I remember the sharpness of her jawline. I remember the innocence behind her eyes resonating with so much emotion that they threatened to burst. But all these memories are a series of fractured pieces that are so much less than Cyren as a whole.

I miss her so much.

She'd know what to say right now. She'd know how to calm my mind. She could always take my swirling thoughts and get them to relax long enough for me to sharpen them, focus them on a single target. We were a perfect team.

I can't accept that Cyren is gone, deleted, dead. I can't accept that the storage space in NextWorld she used to fill is just waiting to be overwritten by some pointless piece of code, some useless data, ones and zeroes that will never add up to anything close to her.

Sleep does finally come, but I don't dream. I fall into a blackness not unlike the game death that robbed me of so much. When I wake, I have no idea what time of day it is. The mirrored screen offers me no information. I stumble around the room, pacing.

I look out the window and watch the trains pass between the towers. I stare at the lights coming from the windows of the neighboring rooms. I let my imagination wander as to who lives behind each glowing square.

Time passes, and sleep comes again. Days go by.

My father returns periodically on his days off. He informs me of his constant struggle to negotiate a plea bargain. He thinks that DOTgov is close to accepting a deal that could grant me probationary access to the communal rooms. Whenever I ask about NextWorld, he always changes the subject. I'm starting to think he doesn't want that restriction removed.

When he turns the conversations to me, he tries to ask me questions about what happened inside the game, but I tell him nothing. It's pointless. There's no way he could understand what I experienced. I doubt he'd believe me. All I'd accomplish is to summon those looks of pity from his eyes. Or maybe it's fear. Or maybe he'd think I'm outright crazy. I mean, I fell in love with an NPC. What father wants to hear *that* from their son?

He's staring directly into my eyes when he asks, "Do you know why I always begged you to spend time with me in the real world?"

I want to mock him. I want to spit out something hurtful that will tell him exactly how little I care about his "real world." I want to tell him that the virus took away the only thing that matters to me.

"It's because I can see her in your eyes."

I glance at him. Something about the way he says it sounds different from his usual speeches. It sounds... *real*.

"The more time passes, the harder it is for me to remember what she looks like. All the digital pictures in the world don't remind me as much as seeing your face."

He reaches out to touch me, but I flinch, pulling away. He doesn't look hurt by my reaction. His hand drops, but he smiles.

"Maybe it was selfish of me," he says. "It just... it made me feel, even if it was for just a brief moment, like she was here again."

When he stands up to leave, I almost say something. I almost tell him I understand. I almost tell him that I'd do anything to see Cyren one last time. I almost tell him that I'm sorry for keeping that from him. But I don't say any of those things. I just watch him leave.

00111101

My father's pleas for leniency in my trial fall upon deaf ears.

The door to my room opens, and he's standing in the doorway next to two DgS officers. Unlike in NextWorld, these officers aren't wearing matching silver suits. Instead, they're clad in navy blue protective armor, wielding batons and wearing helmets with mirrored visors that cover their faces.

The two officers step around my father and approach me. One of them points his baton at me while the other pulls a pair of handcuffs from a pouch on her belt.

"It's okay," my father says as I back away from the two menacing figures. "It's standard procedure. They need to restrain you for transport to the law room."

"It's happening? Now?"

My father nods his head as the DgS officer grabs my wrist and locks the cuff into place. She grabs my shoulder, spins me around, and locks the second cuff on to my other wrist behind my back. With a shove, I stumble out the door. My father catches me.

My paper thin clothes aren't providing me with anything but a modest covering from the cold air of the hallway. My bare feet feel every notch and bump in the ridged metal floor. Everything is too real, too intense, too wild and chaotic. There's no design here.

There's no beauty. It's function over form. The officer gives me another shove to direct me down the hallway.

"Everything will be okay," my father says.

I don't believe him. I don't need his unrealistic words of comfort. I need facts. I need a strategy.

"What are they accusing me of? Tell me what to do. I've never seen a trial before."

My father doesn't make eye contact with me as he speaks. "It doesn't matter what you do. There's nothing we can accomplish at this point. Most likely, they've already made their decision."

I slow my gait to a stunned shuffle. The DgS officer shoves me forward. I stumble, but it forces me to catch up to the conversation.

"What are you talking about? I thought this was my trial."

"In name only."

"You're telling me I'm not going to have a chance to plead my case?"

My father sounds cold and strangely matter-of-fact as he says, "They have to at least pretend to give you the opportunity to represent yourself, but it's for show. They've looked at the data. They already have all the information they need to make their decision. My advice is to say nothing."

"You're telling me that my side of the story doesn't matter at all?"

"Guilty or innocent, the morality of the situation doesn't matter to them. They have a team of experts decide what's best beforehand. They crunch the numbers. They do market research. They decide whether the declaration of your guilt or innocence is best for *them*. You really play no part in what's about to happen."

I raise one brow and look out of the corner of my eyes as I say, "And these are the people you work for?"

"I got into politics to try to fix these problems."

"You aren't doing your job very well."

My father frowns disapprovingly.

It doesn't take long for the super-fast elevator to reach the upper floors of the tower. It still looks drab up here, with the same steel walls as the rest of the tower, but the DOTgov flag hangs on nearly every wall. A red rectangle with a yellow star. Seven smaller stars surround it, each one representing a continent in the global government.

When I was in the elementary years of DOTedu, they forced us to pledge our allegiance to DOTgov every morning. For me, it was just words. A memorized set of sentences that held no meaning. I wasn't disinterested out of a sense of rebellion. I just didn't care. The flag was a boring set of symbols that had always been there.

My father can still remember a time when there was more than one flag, when there was more than one government. He remembers patriotism. He remembers war. He remembers men and women fighting for the world we now live in. To him, the flag means peace. It means unification. It means having hope for our future.

Maybe I take this world for granted. Maybe if I saw how bad it used to be, I'd appreciate what it is now, but it's impossible for me to not see the cracks, the flaws, the things that still need improving.

When we reach the end of the hall, two large doors stand in front of us. A scanner above the door waves a laser over our bodies, communicating with our nanomachines and detecting our identities. When it's finished, the doors slide open, revealing the law room.

The circular room is surprisingly small. Three screens sit across from the doorway, with a camera placed below them. A fourth screen sits off to the right, away from the others. The floor looks like the DOTgov flag. A single bulb rests in the center of the ceiling, with a glowing light beaming directly at the large yellow star on the floor.

The DgS officers push me toward the center of the room and force me to stand in the spotlight. They remain within arm's reach of me, as if I pose some sort of risk.

I glance over my shoulder at my father sitting on a small bench near the door. He gives me a nod of recognition, or maybe it's meant to be encouraging—either way, it angers me. I want him to fight, I want him to save me, but he just sits there, helpless.

The three screens blink to life. An avatar of a judge appears on each one, but each avatar looks exactly the same. I'll never know who condemns me. They're faceless authority figures.

The judge in the middle clears his throat and says, "User name: Arkade. You've been accused of seven counts of cyberterrorism including: inappropriate bandwidth usage, the disruption of network infrastructure, aiding and abetting a known hacker, the exploitation of unstable programming, digital extortion, harboring rogue artificial intelligence, and fraud."

I smirk at the screens and say, "That's all you could come up with? You sure you don't need time to slap some more charges on there?"

The judges all glare at me, but it's the one in the middle who asks, "Are you refusing to confess to these crimes?"

I let out a heavy sigh and say, "Yes. No. Whatever. Let's just get this over with."

The judges glance at each other and the two on either side nod their heads at the one in the middle.

The avatar in the middle bangs a gavel down three times and announces, "The tribunal has officially begun."

00111110

The first stage of the trial consists of the three judges reading obnoxiously long descriptions of legal jargon. They explain each of my crimes in excruciating detail, presumably so that I understand exactly what they're accusing me of and can't later claim any kind of ignorance to the law. This goes on and on until my eyes glaze over with pure boredom.

The second stage utilizes the fourth screen in the room to show a video-cast of different conversations by witnesses. It doesn't take me long to realize that what I'm watching are private conversations, recorded inside NextWorld, unbeknownst to the people involved. Xen and Raev are speaking to each other in a private chat room. Ekko and his partner are talking in DOTsoc. Grael is speaking with his employer in DOTbiz. Klok is discussing what happened to him inside the game world with other players. It's strange, almost voyeuristic, watching their conversations. Everyone knows that privacy doesn't exist inside NextWorld, but seeing the watchful eye of DOTgov firsthand feels wrong, like I should look away out of respect.

They edit descriptions together so that the events play out in a linear fashion, recreating the story from beginning to end. It starts with my entrance into the game with Xen, my meeting with

Fantom, her grouping with Ekko, Klok, and Cyren, the log-out failure, our adventure, and finally my decision to stay in the game world.

When the videos end, the judge in the middle clears his throat and asks, "You'll now have the opportunity to offer your rebuttal to anything said by these eye witnesses."

I glance over my shoulder at my father. He gives a single, firm, shake of his head.

They were telling the truth. All I'd be doing is filling in my point-of-view, which doesn't matter to anyone but me. Should I try to tell them how Cyren makes me feel and how I'd do anything to have that back? Should I explain love to them?

I turn away from my father, toward the judges, and bow my head.

"Very well," the judge says, grumbling with a passive boredom. "We hereby find you guilty on all counts."

My father whimpers behind me. We both know what the punishment is for cyberterrorism. Mind prison. A lifetime spent logged-in to a virtual world devoid of stimuli. Like a sleeping state where you're aware of every second. My hands shake as I face the rest of my life.

"But," the second judge says, "while there is no denying that your actions should suffer severe consequences, we have concluded that we should also take into account the age at which you made these decisions."

I look up. A moment of hope. A moment where I think they might let me go. A moment where I think that I might see the virtual world again.

The third judge leans back in his chair and says, "By all accounts, you were a child when you committed these crimes. A child that was so obsessed, so addicted to these... *games* that he was willing to do anything to keep playing them. You're sick... not evil."

"Therefore," the first judge speaks up again, "we have chosen to forgo the usual punishment. We will still place you on the DOTgov cyberterrorist list and deny you access to any form of digital communications for the remainder of your life, but instead of serving the usual prison sentence, we will be placing you in a rehabilitation facility until an expert panel deems you fit to return to your tower."

The judge slams his gavel down and the screens go black. The tight grip of the two DgS officers wrap around my skinny forearms and yank me toward the door. My father hurries behind me.

"You did well, son. We couldn't have expected a better outcome than that. You should consider yourself very lucky."

"Lucky?"

I try to swim through my disillusionment as the officers force me into an elevator. Before long, they're shoving me on to my bed face first and roughly unlocking the handcuffs. They disappear out the door without a word, leaving me alone with my father.

"I wish there was more I could do," he says, his voice sounding like a light breeze. "I wanted—"

"You got what you wanted," I say, cutting him off.

He reaches toward me and says, "It's for the best. Before you know it you'll be back in your old room and we can meet every day in the tower communal area and—"

"I'm tired."

He rubs his tongue against his gums and says, "Sure. Of course. I'll be back before they... I'll see you before you go."

I curl up on the bed in the fetal position, like I used to do inside the E-Womb. I hear the door hiss shut as my father leaves the room. When he does, I roll over and stare at the ceiling.

I don't know how to handle what's inside of me. When I watched those videos, it made me realize how much I took my friends for granted. Now that I know I may never see them again, it's like DOTgov has stolen more of my heart. It doesn't matter if they lock me in a mind prison, or a rehab center, or my own tower room. Any life without Cyren is going to be empty.

As these thoughts consume me, I notice my vision blur and wobble. I rub my eyes and see a flicker when I open them, as if my brain was experiencing bandwidth lag for a moment. Then text appears in front of me, not on a screen, but in front of my face, floating inches from my eyes. One letter after another, as if I'm watching someone type in real time.

"Arkade?"

I wave my hand in the air, trying to swat at the word in front of me. My hand passes right through the letters. I rub my eyes with the tips of my fingers again, but when I shut my eyelids, the letters are still there.

"What is this?" I mumble to myself.

The letters spelling out my name in front of me disappear and the words "I can hear you" appear in their place.

I look around, expecting to see someone else in the room, but no one is there. Have I finally lost it? Am I going crazy? Or is this some kind of feedback, a flashback from being logged-in for so long?

Words type in front of me again: "I have input access to your retinal nanomachines and output access to your vocal nanomachines. You can see what I type, and I can hear what you say."

I open my mouth to reply, but I stop myself, afraid to say anything. Is this some kind of joke? Who would have access to my nanomachines remotely? That's impossible. Isn't it?

"Give me a second. I'll get you out of there."

Could DOTgov be doing this? Maybe they're testing me. Maybe they're trying to see if I'm going to be a flight risk or not. There's a large *clunk* as the lock on my tower room door releases.

The text reads, "Follow the arrow."

A glowing arrow appears in front of me as if it were lying on the floor, pointing toward the tower room door.

"I'm not going anywhere," I say, confident in the fact that I'm calling DOTgov's bluff.

"Yes. You are. Now move!"

"How are you doing this?" I ask, reaching out and trying to touch the words again, amazed by whatever technology is making this possible.

The words appear across my vision quickly, like the sender is furiously typing them. They fill my entire vision. "Really? Is that really what you want to talk about right now? Do you want me to explain how I reversed the I/O protocols of the tower nanomachine scanners so that instead of a read-only format they can send write commands? Or do you want to follow that arrow I'm displaying on the floor and log back into NextWorld?"

I glance at the door when the words disappear. "Why should I do anything that you're saying?"

"Because," the words type, slower and more thoughtful this time, "Cyren hasn't been deleted yet."

I stand up. The words floating in the air are burning into my eyes. They remain in the same position, almost mocking me with their simplicity. I want to reach out and hold them, to pull them closer so they can make me safe again.

I try to reply, to form words when my thoughts are nothing but a whirlwind, but I only manage to stammer, "Wh-who... who are you?"

The answer appears in front of me: "A friend."

00111111

As soon as I step out the door, a sense of freedom washes over me. It isn't a singular sensation. The openness of possibilities mixes with my extreme loneliness. The empty hallway shatters the safety that the monotony of my disconnected tower room brought me. I'm exposed. At any moment a camera or a sensor or a real person could see me and bring this all to a tragic end. Then I think of what the words said.

"Cyren hasn't been deleted yet."

It's all I need to press on. I follow the glowing arrow toward my goal. When I reach the end of the hall, I hear the door of one of the tower rooms open behind me.

"Quick! Open the hatch!" appears in the air.

On the wall there is a label on a small door that reads "Waste Disposal." I cringe at the thought of what's inside, but when I hear a voice coming from the open doorway of the tower room behind me, the sound forces my hand. The hatch lets out a gaseous release of air when it unseals and the smell almost knocks me from my feet.

"Get inside."

I reread the words and wait for the sender to retype them, assuming there must be a mistake.

When the arrow points at the opening, I whisper, "Are you serious?"

"This is the only way. Go. Now."

I glance back at the doorway and see a figure emerge. My instinctual need to hide pushes me through the small opening. I have to stop my body from sliding down the chamber, the walls slick with an unknown slime. There's a trickling stream of liquid constantly running between my fingertips. I press my hands firmly against the metal, trying to keep myself from falling through the angled shaft. The glowing arrow points upward.

"You need to climb."

I let out an already-exhausted gasp of air and push myself upward. My fingers and toes press hard against one wall, with my back shoved against the other. Loose screws and bolts scrape against me, tearing my flesh. Combined with the foul smell of the vapors inside the chamber, I'm reminded of how awful reality can be.

I'm not sure how far I make it before my arms shake, threatening to give out and drop me down the metal shaft.

"You can do this."

"No," I say through gritted teeth. "I can't."

"You have to."

I want to argue. I want to give up. I want to crawl back out of the hatch and hide inside my room, but I think of Cyren. I think of her rippling muscles, and her black lips, and her defiance that would never allow her to give up if I were the one in danger. My arms stiffen with a new resolve and I inch myself upward.

It feels like hours pass. The words in front of me intermittently provide messages of encouragement. When I shut my eyes, the arrow and the text appear inside my eyelids, streaming straight to my retinas.

"You're almost there. You should see a mesh wire covering the opening to a horizontal shaft just above you."

Sure enough, a few feet above me the glowing arrow points at a ventilation shaft. Warm air blows across the sewage drain. My legs shove upward and I'm looking into the blowing breeze, enjoying the heated air as it tickles my shivering skin.

I stick my fingers through the wire cover and yank on it as hard as I can. The cage-like fence bends outward before popping free. I let it drop down the shaft. It sends a loud scraping noise echoing through the chamber as it falls past each floor. With a final heave, I manage to wedge my elbows inside the opening and lift the rest of my body inside. My arms and legs melt on to the floor, every muscle accepting my weakness.

"You need to keep moving."

"I can't," I say, barely able to catch enough breath to speak.

"Opening your door alerted security."

"Give me a second."

"We don't have a second. It will only be a matter of time before they send search drones into the ventilation shafts."

"Where am I going? What's your plan? I can't go through any checkpoints without them scanning my nanomachines. They'll find me eventually."

"We need to get you to another tower so you can get aboard a train."

My eyes blink open. I've never been on a train before. Not in the real world. I've never wanted to go anywhere that would require that kind of transportation.

"Where are you taking me?"

"Somewhere safe."

"What does that mean?"

"You'll be in NextWorld eventually. That's all that matters."

They're right. Whoever is sending this text is speaking to me in a logical way that I can appreciate. It doesn't leave any room for doubt. I push forward. Like a machine.

The heat of the ventilation shaft is nice at first, but soon my body is sweating. My skin swells. My lips grow chapped and my mouth dries out. I'm scampering through the shaft, trying to get to my destination quicker.

When I see an opening in the floor of the shaft ahead of me, I move faster. I press my face against the metal cage that covers the opening, trying to suck in some of the colder air from outside.

"Back up!" appears in front of my face, but the cool air feels so good that I ignore it.

"It's that politician's kid," I hear a voice say from directly below me.

I open my eyes and look down on a group of five armed officers from the DgS. The visors that normally shield their faces are casually raised as they talk to each other.

"You mean that twerp that logged-in to that game for all those years?"

"That's the one."

"You realize they've been paying for that kid to play games all day with our global credit budget?"

"Oh, I know. I've been telling my partner for years that they should just unplug him and see what happens."

"That'd fry his nanomachines."

"Who cares? Just because his father is some kind of bigwig in DOTgov, that don't mean he should get any kind of special treatment. What do you think they would do if one of *our* kids got trapped in there? They'd turn them into a vegetable before we knew what was what."

"Still don't make it right."

I'm so lost in the conversation that I don't realize how much of my sweat is dripping through the mesh wire covering. A rather large droplet hangs from the tip of my nose, but before I can wipe it away, it breaks loose and plops on to one of the officer's forehead. She looks startled for a moment and when she peers up to see where the drip came from, I push myself away from the opening. I think I move quickly enough for her not to see me, but the sudden shift of my weight makes the thin metal bend underneath me.

The text changes to "GO! GO! GO!"

I lunge down the chamber on my hands and knees as I hear one of the officers yell out, "He's in the ventilation shaft!"

01000000

I can hear shouting through the metal walls of the ventilation shaft. Security guards are yelling at each other in the hallway below me. They're trying to follow my movements, trying to figure out where I'm going to end up. It sounds far from organized. Some of them think I'm heading toward higher levels. Some of them think I'm heading toward lower levels. When they decide on their own courses of action, they spread out in multiple directions.

"You're lucky."

"No matter how many times people try to tell me that, I still don't believe it."

"You're going to be a lot less lucky if those guards catch you."

I can't argue with that.

At the end of another long chamber, there is a large fan spinning, cutting through the beams of light from the other side. There are no other chambers leading off of this one.

"Now what?" I say, annoyed that the glowing arrow led me down a dead end.

"Keep going."

"I can't. There's a fan blocking my path."

"Go through it."

I actually laugh. It's a cold, dark laugh, but it's still odd. I'm not sure I remember the last time I laughed. Not in the real world anyway.

"I *can't* go through it. The fan is active. I mean, if I go through it, this conversation is going to get cut short. Along with my neck."

"It's timing."

"Timing?"

"Think of it like a game. The blade rotation isn't random. Just time your movements."

"You're insane. I'm not going to—"

I hear a buzzing sound behind me. The noise is bouncing off the metal interior of the ventilation shaft, making it impossible for me to gauge how far away it actually is.

"Drones," I whisper.

"You need to move. Now."

I look back at the fan and curse under my breath. This isn't a game. This isn't fun. This is real life, and I hate it.

The closer I get to the blades, the more they blur together. The heat is blowing right in my face, making my eyes water. I look down at the bottom edge of the circular opening, trying to focus on each singular blade as it swoops past. I try to count, to find the pause between each rotation, but it's too fast. There's no way I'm going to fit my entire body through the gap.

"I can't do this."

"You have to."

The buzzing sound from behind me grows louder. A small machine floats around the corner. Four propellers keep it aloft and a bright light sits under the front-mounted camera. It points directly at me.

"Go!"

I turn back to the fan, trying to push myself forward, to summon the bravery to leap through the decapitating machine, but I can't. My brain won't let me. It's impossible.

The drone slides through the ventilation shaft with ease. Its approach is calculated, zooming in on my image. It stops a few feet away, keeping me centered in the camera's view.

I glance at the fan, then back at the drone. With a quick lunge, I grip on to the sides of the drone and yank it toward me. The propellers spin faster as it tries to fly away from me, but I don't give it the chance. I throw it the other way, toward the fan. The large blades hack through one of the drone's propellers and tear it off. The fan drags the body of the drone with the rotation, wedging it inside the track of the fan's blades. The fan screeches to a halt. I don't hesitate. I jump through the stalled blades. As soon as I'm on the other side, the fan manages to rip the drone free and continue spinning.

"Nicely done."

I exhale and say, "Two birds. One stone."

The arrow leads me through more of the maze of ventilation shafts until I reach another mesh wire opening. I approach it slowly and peer through the cage. It looks out into a huge vertical chamber with tracks running up and down the walls. I'm not sure what I'm looking at until an elevator rushes past at an incredible speed. Another one drops down the other side.

"We need to get you to the upper floors."

"You want me to take an elevator?"

"You can't go inside them. They'll scan your nanomachines."

"So what do you want me to do?"

The dramatic pause before the text appears makes me nervous. For good reason.

"You need to jump on top."

"Okay," I say leaning back. "I had a hunch when you tried to get me to jump through that fan, but now I'm sure of it. You're trying to kill me."

"There's no other way to go up."

"Then I guess we're done. I lose."

"If I thought giving up or losing was an option for you, I wouldn't have tried."

Another elevator rushes past the opening. The entire ventilation shaft shakes.

"If one of those things hits me, I'm going to be a stain. A big red stain."

"You need to be smart about it."

"Going anywhere near that opening is probably the stupidest thing I could do."

"You're wasting time. Time that Cyren doesn't have."

I clench my fist and bang it on the metal wall. Seeing her name causes such an emotional upheaval inside me that even if there was a slight chance of saving her, I'd be willing to throw myself down the shaft and just hope I land on my feet. Whoever is sending this text knows that.

I push my face against the mesh wire and watch another elevator rush past, speeding upward like a rocket. Another elevator drops toward the lower levels at the same speed. My gamer brain clicks in. Strategies flow through me. Calculations and patterns.

"If I step on to an elevator lifting into the air, I'm going to die. It will splatter me. But if I drop on to an elevator that's lowering... I should catch up to it and land softly." I shut my eyes, not believing the words coming out of my mouth. "I hope."

"Now you're using your brain."

"No. My brain is telling me to stop listening to you. This is my stupid, stupid heart talking."

I shuffle around inside the tight chamber until my legs are in front of me. With a few swift kicks, I manage to knock the covering off the opening. I watch as it falls down the elevator shaft, disappearing into the bottomless pit. I look up, waiting to see an elevator approaching. One rushes past, but I hesitate too long. Luckily I manage to stop myself from leaping out. If I don't time it correctly, I'm going to fall too far, too fast, and slam into the top of the elevator.

A big red stain.

Another elevator drops toward me and I count silently. One, two, three. When the roof passes by, I shut my eyes, picture Cyren's smile, and jump out into the open air.

It's much cooler in the elevator shaft, which is a nice feeling as I plummet to my death. The cold is surging past me. I try to take a breath, but I can't breathe. There's too much pressure on my chest. Is that panic? I'm going to die. What did I do? What was I thinking?

Ten, twenty, thirty floors rush past. The minimal lighting blurs together as my speed builds. The details of my death become a stream of color and sound that detaches me from what I'm doing.

I force the panic out of my head and start to think straight. Rolling in mid-air, I tuck my legs under me. My toes touch something. It's the metal roof of the elevator, descending right below me. We've been dropping at the same speed, but it's slowing down. My feet press down on the roof. My heels set down. My knees gradually bend, allowing my weightless body to grip on to the ridged metal. It takes another twenty floors, but eventually gravity returns and I settle on to the roof. When I stop moving completely, my lungs heave, taking in quick, strained breaths. Between the tiny, frenzied gasps of air, I manage to read the text floating in front of me.

"Wow. I can't believe that worked."

I'm about to yell out at the text when the elevator surges into motion. The speed flattens me against the roof when the elevator lifts upward. The rush is so intense that I have to close my eyes and pretend I'm somewhere else. Thankfully, it doesn't last long. The elevator slows, just like it did when going down.

"Okay. This floor should work."

The glowing arrow appears again, pointing at another hatch. There's a label, but it's old and faded. I can't read any of the print below the word: "Warning."

"What is this?"

"It's an emergency release valve. In case the elevator shaft ever got flooded."

"I don't understand," I say, squinting my eyes and trying to read the label again. "Where does it go?"

Even when I read the text for a second time, I don't believe what I'm seeing.

"It goes outside."

01000001

"We don't have time to argue." The text appears while I'm yelling objections at it. "This elevator isn't going to sit here and wait for you."

I slam my hand against the warning label and yell, "Why are you doing this to me?"

"Because it's the only way out."

"I'll die."

"No, you won't."

"It's the outside!"

"You won't be out there long."

"No!" I yell, then in a whisper I say, "I'm scared."

"Trust me. I've gotten you this far."

"No, *I've* gotten me this far. You've just been directing me toward one death trap after another."

"I never said it would be easy."

"But—"

"Cyren can't afford the time we're wasting."

I take a deep breath, trying to bottle my fear as I grit my teeth and pull the lever on the hatch. The door swings open with a loud, wrenching creak, like no one has oiled it in decades. Inside is a long, dark tube, rusted and unused. I crawl inside, but my shoulder width barely fits. I have to wrestle to get my entire body inside. A panicked sense of claustrophobia tries to back me out, but I close my eyes and force myself deeper. Once I'm a few yards in, all I can see is the text, hovering inside my eyes.

"A hundred yards."

"Is that all?"

I wiggle and worm my way through every yard, like vitapaste trying to free itself from the tube. Eventually I spot a point of light in the distance. It grows with every push forward, beckoning me closer. By the time I get near, I see a yellow utility bulb over yet another hatch. I wrestle my arm out from under my body and grab on to the handle.

"Wait!" appears in front of me.

"What now?"

"That's the last door before you're outside."

I pull my hand away.

"There are no sensors outside the tower, so I'm going to lose contact with your nanomachines, but it's okay. Follow the ledge to your right, cross the train bridge, and enter the hatch in the adjoining tower."

"Right," I say with a derisive huff, "sounds easy."

"Try not to breathe too deeply."

"Sounds like good advice."

I place both hands on the release lever and fill my lungs with filtered air. With a jerk, I pull the lever free and the hatch flings open. The sudden suction of air nearly pulls me from the tube, flinging me into the open sky, but I manage to brace both hands on either side of the opening to stop myself. I try to move quickly, stepping out on to the small ledge and turning to the right. Even though I know I should, I can't stop myself from looking down.

Hundreds of towers, staggered in sizes, are around me. The top of each one is in a perpetual state of construction, always adding another level to accommodate the growing population. A million flashing lights and glowing windows scatter across my view. Cords and wires and tubes hang slack between each building, an interwoven mess of electricity and digital connectivity. I can't see the earth. It makes my stomach spin. The dizziness sways me forward. My hands grip tightly to the side of the building. I force myself to look away from the death below. Gray clouds blanket the city, lightning bolts constantly dancing in flaring arcs across them.

A destroyed atmosphere with nothing left to do but scream out in pain.

I'm lost in the immensity of everything when a train rumbles past, shaking the building that I'm clinging to. The small ledge my heels are on vibrates. I press my back to the wall, trying to stay firmly in place. When the movement settles, I shift my body, making my way to the right. I can't help thinking of the cliff side in the Darkfyre Mountains and my group's nearly fatal fall. I survived it then, but I don't have a magic belt to save me this time.

As I pass the window next to me glowing with a plate of artificial sunlight, I feel the first effects of the outside air. My eyes water, a burning sensation piercing straight through them. I let go of the wall with one hand and rub them, but it doesn't help. Tears stream down my face. My skin itches. It's like stepping through a fog of acid, a chemical bath in an ocean of corrosive liquids.

My feet move faster as my lungs struggle to hold on to the air inside me. I pass three more windows before I reach the train bridge between the two buildings. I can't take it anymore. My chest heaves, letting out all the breath I've been saving. I try not to inhale, but my body demands it. It burns worse on the inside. The air tears apart my throat before my lungs are filled with burning coals.

My eyes are watering so much by this point that I can barely see. The bridge is right below me, but judging the distance I have to drop is impossible. I wipe the tears from my face and squint, trying to focus. It looks like ten feet, but it could be twenty for all I know. I look back at the hatch I came out of, hesitating for a moment.

I shimmy over the side of the ledge and lower myself down as much as I can. My fingers grip on to the metal ridge and my body dangles freely. My arms cry out in pain, knowing they can't suspend my weight. I close my eyes and let go.

It feels like forever, falling through the open air of the city, but I eventually slam on to the bridge. My legs crumple underneath me and my back slaps against the magnetic rails. It forces me to suck in more air. I lurch forward, hacking and coughing violently. I cover my mouth with my hand and when I pull it away I can see specks of red against my pale skin.

I lift myself off the tracks, my muscles aching, my back swelling with pain, my legs shaking weakly. I'm trying to give myself time to limp forward, but the bridge rumbles underneath me. I look over my shoulder and see two beams of light round the corner of a building far in the distance. I start jogging, but the light is gaining on me. I force myself into an all-out run for the end of the bridge. The tracks shake more and more as I near the next building. I can hear the rattle and hum of the magnetic thrusters hunting me down like prey.

When I reach the other side of the bridge, I frantically search the walls for another hatch. A few feet from the edge there is a small circle with the same faded warning label. I lunge for it, gripping the handle with both hands and pulling, but it doesn't budge. It feels welded shut, like the corrosive atmosphere has melted the door to its frame. I look over my shoulder and see the train reach the bridge. My eyes dart around, looking for somewhere safe to hide, but there's only the edge that drops off into the emptiness between the towers. I have two choices. I either die instantly upon impact, or I die hundreds of stories below. I choose neither.

I grip on to the handle again, leaping into the air and using my weight to pull down. My shoulder dislocates, but the lever also loosens and turns. I throw the hatch open and leap inside, pulling my legs in close to my chest as the train reaches me. The door breaks loose from its hinges when the train slams into it and roars past.

My entire body burns with pain, but I lurch deeper into the tube, pulling myself with one arm. The deeper I go, the cleaner the air feels. My nanomachines work faster and faster, trying to clean the cells I've destroyed in the last few minutes. The microscopic tools numb my shoulder and focus my vision.

"I knew you could do it," the text reads as it twitches back into view.

Through a fit of coughing, I barely manage to say, "That makes one of us."

01000010

The end of the tube opens into a hallway that looks empty, so I drop down to the floor and close the hatch behind me. The glowing arrow rounds the second corner to the right.

"The train station is nearby," the text reads. "They won't be looking for you in this tower, but you still need to be careful not to get scanned."

I stumble forward, my legs feeling better with every step I take. When I make a few turns through the tower, I see a crowd of people at the end of a wide hall riding an escalator upward. A sign at the top reads: Departure Station. A family hurries past me, late for their train. I nonchalantly merge with the crowd, trying to act like I belong. Men and women, adults and children. Pale, hairless skin hanging on differently shaped bodies.

It's strange, being around this many real people. The smell of their sweat and the gruffness of their movements as they push and shove their way past each other. My breathing becomes quick gasps of air. My heartbeat races. Their mere presence is crushing me. The sheer number of them around me suffocates the air from the room. It's too much. It's too real.

When I reach the top of the escalator, I rush to the side of the train station, trying to find a corner to catch my breath. I lean against a large screen displaying DOTcom advertisements. The citizens walking past me give me a quick glance as I hunch over, sucking in air like I'm drowning, but they move on just as fast, forgetting the strange sight.

"Stay in the crowd," the text reads.

"There are too many of them."

"And one of you. Which makes you stand out."

"How do you plan on getting me aboard a train? I can't just buy a ticket."

"You won't need a ticket."

"You need a ticket to board a train."

"Not every train."

The arrow flashes on the floor, leading me back into the sea of people. I take a few more deep breaths and push off from the commercial screen, wading into the current of smells and sounds and jerking elbows. Train whistles blow from the tracks, alarms sound in the distance, and the speaker system periodically announces routine instructions for boarding times. I try to drown out the blanket of stimuli and focus on the arrow. I'm bounced back and forth between bodies going in different directions, but I plant my feet hard against the floor and manage to work through the crowd, crossing the entire expanse of the station.

The arrow points at a door that clearly reads: Maintenance Only.

"How am I supposed to—"

"Wait."

My eyes dart around, watching the faces of every passerby, trying to determine their level of suspicion. To the left and to the right, over and over. A hundred faces pass by. No one notices me. They're too involved in their own lives, their own destinations.

But then I see a security guard. I press up against the wall next to the door, wishing there was a shadow to cover me, a hatch to crawl inside, something that would shield me from the guard's eyes.

"Wait" is all that appears in front of me.

"I can't," I say, pushing off from the wall, back into the crowd. "He's going to see me."

The guard stops a man next to him for a routine scan of his nanomachine signature. I try to imagine what I'm going to say if he catches me. Could I pretend I'm lost? Could I pretend this was all a big accident?

The maintenance door next to me opens.

A worker steps out carrying a large bag.

"Now!" appears in front of me.

I grab the side of the door before it swings shut and slide inside. There's a long hallway stretching either way, lined with lockers.

"Nice job" appears in front of me.

My breathing is erratic. I don't know if I should relax now that I'm away from the guard and the crowds, or panic because I'm in an even more dangerous area.

"This place is restricted," I whisper through clenched teeth. "If I get caught—"

"You're a cyberterrorist now. Everywhere is restricted."

The arrow points down the hall, to the right. I hustle past the lockers and turn into a doorway on the far end. I step onto a balcony that overlooks a large factory. Steam rises from vents all over the floor, masking the true size of the room. I can see large robotic arms picking up seven-foot long containers from a conveyor belt and loading them on to a train.

"What is this?"

The arrow continues to flash, pointing down a stairway that leads to the factory floor. I look over the railing, but I don't see anyone around, so I make my way over to one of the stacks. When I reach it, the arrow disappears.

"Open it," the text reads.

"The container?"

There's no response, which I take as a confirmation. I search the outside of the container, and when I find the latch, I also find a label. There's a bunch of shipping information on it, but underneath it reads: Contents - Vitapaste.

I lift the latch and the top of the container flips open automatically. The substance fills the interior like a coffin of cold, gray goo.

"What am I supposed to do with this?"

"Get inside."

I look around, wondering again if this is all some kind of sick joke. Is it too late to back out? I stick my hand in the vitapaste, testing it. It's cold and grainy. I shiver.

"How am I supposed to breathe?"

"Get inside."

I want to slap the words from my view, but instead I follow the directions. I have to accept this new reality. The text has gotten me this far and I have no other option. I'm past the point of no return. *Far* past it.

I step into the vitapaste, lifting the rest of my body over the edge. I lower myself into the gelatinous texture, inch-by-inch, trying to allow my body time to adjust to the temperature. It's no use. My teeth are already chattering. My muscles are shivering. The vitapaste spills over the side as my body displaces the volume.

A yellow light flashes on the wall next to the stack of containers. I hear a whistle. I lean up and look over the edge as one of the robotic arms swivels toward me. It reaches down and scans the container next to me. Once it reads the bar code on the label, it lifts the container from the floor and sets it on the next car of the train. When it releases the container, it turns back toward me. I grab the lid, slamming it shut on top of me.

I'm left in darkness. I can barely hear the outside, but soon enough the container lifts from the floor and slams on to the bed of the train. The vitapaste sloshes around on top of me. I wait in the silent, cold darkness for what feels like forever before I hear another alarm and the movement of the train.

"You did it," the text reads.

"Yeah," I say, spitting vitapaste from my mouth. "I'm in a coffin of vitapaste. This isn't exactly what you promised me, is it? I thought you were getting me back in to NextWorld."

"The train will deliver you to a tower in the twenty-four million district. Old Mongolia."

"Mongolia?" It's hard for me to comprehend the distance from my tower in Old Russia. "What's in Mongolia?"

"Your new E-Womb. It's time for us to meet."

01000011

The train ride takes hours. I manage to sleep, but it's restless. All I dream about is Cyren, trapped in a world of empty blackness or swallowed by the virus, deleted from the world I'd have given anything to protect.

I'm angry because she should have trusted me. I'm angry because she should have given me a chance to come up with a plan. But then I fall in love with her all over again when I remember that everything she did was to save me. She put my life ahead of her own. They all did. The NPCs knew we were going to die. They knew it was only a matter of time. Who knows what would have happened if that virus deleted me? Would it have corrupted my nanomachines? DOTgov says that's impossible, they say NextWorld is perfectly safe, but I've already proven that wrong. What else are they lying about?

I'm woken from my dreams and nightmares as something lifts my cargo container from the train. It shakes and rumbles as it's set down, splashing the gray liquid around me. My fingers trace the inside edge of the container until I find a release lever. I throw the latch and the lid springs open. I suck in fresher air than the stagnant combination of the sweat and vitapaste aroma inside. My eyes blink a few times to adjust to the light, but when they do, I see the inside of another warehouse.

Huge stacks of vitapaste containers, like towers themselves, lay in rows as far as I can see. Robotic arms are sorting each container, setting them inside the tubes that will deliver the different assortment of nutrients to the tower rooms that require them.

I lift myself out of the container, the vitapaste making a sucking noise as it releases me from its viscous grasp. Some of the goo drips from my body in clumps, but most of it hangs on, stuck to my skin like dried clay.

I look around for a moment, lost in the hugeness of everything, but soon enough the glowing arrow appears in front of me.

"Almost there."

It's simple, but encouraging. I have to get out of this place. The cold temperatures. The loud noises. The horrific smells. The bland tastes. The abrasive textures. The constant threat of someone finding me. I need an E-Womb. I need NextWorld. I need Cyren.

I slap my vitapaste-covered feet against the steel flooring of the warehouse, jogging past rows of containers and dodging the swinging robotic arms. I follow the arrow through the maze of containers until it reaches a far wall, but the arrow doesn't stop. It continues upward, running the height of the wall before streaming into another air duct near the sixty-foot tall ceiling.

When I get close to the wall, I search for steps, a ladder, or handholds, but there is nothing. The wall is sheer metal. It looks as if someone constructed it from a single sheet, devoid of seams or rivets.

"Now what?"

"Follow the arrow."

Is the text trying to mock me?

"How am I supposed to walk up a wall?"

There's no reply.

"Are you just torturing me now?"

"No," the text appears large in the center of my view. "I believe in you more than you do. I'm more confident than you that you can solve a puzzle this simple."

I let out an exhausted breath and grumble to myself. No real words spin inside my throat, just an upset noise that mimics some kind of animal.

I'm angry because the text is right. I've grown soft and complacent. The game world was too easy. Maximum Level. Nearly every magic item. Now it's just me and the real world. No Level progression. No magic items. It's my own body. My own spindly muscles. My own soft flesh and brittle bones. The only thing I still have is my mind. That's stronger than any metal. Sharper than any blade. Faster than any bullet.

I scan the surroundings and see a robotic arm swing overhead. It picks up a container of vitapaste and sets it on a conveyor belt. Then it returns to the same stack of containers and grabs another. Each time, it just misses a second robotic arm reaching for a completely different stack. This stack is much higher, and this robotic arm swings past the air duct that my flashing arrow is pointing at. I watch the mechanical dance for a few moments, counting in my head, keeping beat with my foot.

When I have the pattern down, I wrap my hands around the edges of the vitapaste container next to me and scurry up the side of the stack. I'm only a few feet off the ground and already my arms are shaking, my legs quivering underneath me. They're tired. They threaten to give up and drop me to the floor where they can rest again, but my mind refuses to let them. I push myself past the point of exhaustion. Each time I lift a limb, I groan and scream, doing everything I can to elevate myself a few more feet. When I reach the top of the stack, I hook my jaw on the corner of the top container. It gives me a moment to rest before I get my elbow over the edge to lift the rest of my body.

I pant and wheeze. My chest rises and each time it does, my ribs want to shatter and burst through my skin. My lungs want to shrivel to deflated bags of flesh. My arms twitch, my muscles torn inside. My legs ache with a cramped stiffness from overuse. I feel as if I may die right there, lost in the mechanical gears of the tower's inner workings.

But I don't die. I'm thrust back into movement when the robotic arm swings overhead and descends right at me. Its clawed hand opens to grab the container I'm laying on. I roll to the side before the palm of the claw crushes me, wrapping my arms around the metal beam that carries the container into the air.

When it reaches the apex of its movement, it comes to a sudden halt that shakes me so hard I nearly lose my grip. My mind holds strong, pushing my arms into whatever reserve of strength they might still hold. The metal arm pivots, swinging me and the container through the air. I squint my eyes, searching my surroundings for the other robotic arm, but when I find it, it's too late. The second robotic arm swings past at such a fast speed that it's already descending toward the next container.

I close my eyes and count, replaying the pattern that the robotic arms follow in my head. When I reach the count of forty-five, I let go, allowing the momentum of the swing to throw me into the open air. I open my eyes in time to slam into the second robotic arm and dig my fingers into an open tangle of cords. The arm swings and I dangle behind it, holding on with one hand. The cords pull loose with my weight hanging from them, but they catch at the last moment, providing me with the next seven seconds that I need.

I hit fifty-two in my mental countdown and I let go of the cords. My body is flung through the air and I strike the air duct hard. The covering caves in. My ankle slams into the edge of the opening and I tumble into the corridor.

When my eyes flutter open, the pain in my body alerts me to its presence. Blood trickles on to my foot. My ankle is throbbing. My head is pounding. My limbs feel like they're missing the bones inside. I'm sprawled on the floor of the air duct without the ability to move.

My nanomachines kick in, distributing painkillers to my ankle and head. They mend the open flesh on my ankle, but I'll still have a scar. They stimulate my muscles, helping me lift myself off the metal flooring and look around.

"Nice job" appears in front of me, and the flashing arrow continues down the metal shaft.

I don't say anything. I keep moving before my mind can think about giving up. On my hands and knees, I move as fast as I can. I'm not sure how far I travel. I take an endless amount of lefts and rights and ups and downs through the maze of ventilation before the arrow stops over a single opening in the floor of the air duct. A bright circle is pulsating over the metal grate.

"This is it," appears in front of me.

A sudden surge pushes me toward the opening. I peer through the grate and see a family tower room below me. Larger than my single room, it's made for two partners and a child.

"What are you waiting for?"

I bang my fists on the metal grate, but only manage to bend the metal slightly. I shift my body around in the ventilation shaft and slam my feet against the covering. It doesn't do anything to alleviate the pain in my ankle, but after six hits the metal grate still doesn't break free. I almost laugh when I consider my luck if I'm stopped this close to my destination.

That's when someone steps into view. I lurch backward, filled with panic at the sight, but the man below me reaches toward the ventilation grate. He releases some kind of fastening on the other side and removes the cover.

I'm a few feet away from the opening, but I'm frozen in place. I can't move, hoping with all my might that he didn't see me, didn't hear me.

"Arkade?"

The voice doesn't sound familiar.

"Arkade?" the person says again. "It's okay. You can come down."

I move toward the opening and look down at the man below. He's smiling back at me. He offers me his hand. I'm still moving slowly, reaching out inch by inch toward him. I'm waiting for him to snag me and yank me from the shaft, only to put handcuffs on me, but none of that happens. The man grips me and lowers me to the floor. I scan the room for others, but no one else is there. I look up at the man. He's still smiling.

He must read the confusion on my face because he apologetically holds up his hands and says, "Sorry! You have no idea who I am, do you?"

"Were you the one sending me the text?"

The man tilts his head. Now he looks as confused as me. "No... I..." He smiles again and holds out his hand to greet me, "I'm Ekko's partner."

The acknowledgment of the name floods through my entire body. I crumple to the floor, holding back my need to weep. The man crouches down next to me, reaching out to wrap his arm around my shoulders, but he stops himself when he realizes how disgusting I smell. I can't blame him.

"You look like you could use a shower."

I shake my head, unwilling to explain to him how little the smell of this physical body means to me. "There's no time for that."

"Hey, kiddo, it's okay. Everything is going to be okay."

I rub my forehead and ask, "If it wasn't you that was sending me the text, then—"

"Not sure," he says. "Ekko told me this morning that he got a message saying you'd be coming to visit. I have to admit, I thought you'd be using the door."

"Where's Ekko?"

He points at one of the three E-Wombs and says, "Working. He's usually gone long hours so that we can afford to keep our family room until DOTgov renews our child license."

I glance at the third E-Womb built into the wall.

"It's all yours," he says, motioning to the machine. When I glance back at him with a confused look he says, "Ekko said you'd be pretty anxious to log-in."

I struggle to stand up. I also struggle to make sense of the situation.

"Th-thank you."

He gives me an even bigger smile and says, "You saved my partner's life. This is the least we can do for you."

I step toward the E-Womb, unsure if my actions are inappropriate or rude. Am I supposed to say more to this person I've never met before? I look back at him, but he motions toward the machine again.

"What are you waiting for?"

I don't waste any more time worrying about social interactions. I stick my finger into the small opening with the vitapaste sensor and wait for the door to open and offer me a tube of the gray goo. When it does, I squirt the entire tube into my mouth, letting the excess hang from the corners of my lips. I nearly choke trying to swallow it all, but once it's down, I open the E-womb next to me and crawl into the spherical chamber. I give a wave of thanks to Ekko's partner one last time as the door closes behind me. The interior lights turn on and the machine hums as the electrical heat cradles me.

"Log-in," I say.

The white light flashes and I leave my body. I leave the pain, and the cold, and the weakness.

The pixels of NextWorld shimmer into view all around me, surrounding me with a view that comes into focus rather fast. I'm sitting on a wooden bench in the middle of a very plain, very empty park. Whoever designed it couldn't have spent more than an hour on it. Trees lacking any detail spot the landscape in patterned positions. The lawn is a solid green, without any actual blades of grass. The readouts in my view tell me I'm in DOTorg. The space is misspelled: Momm laand 43b. It's exactly the kind of place someone would overlook in a list, which makes me wonder if this series of indistinct design choices could be intentional.

When I hear someone approaching from behind, I spin into a defensive stance, forgetting I don't have any weapons or defenses in this world to protect me. Behind me there's an avatar I haven't seen in a long time. She's wrapped in a white kimono with yellow floral patterns. She's wearing her white hair in pigtails tied back with ribbons of the same yellow as the floral pattern. The only difference from the last time I saw her is the lack of a giant sword strapped to her back and the fact that her white face-paint is now marked in the shape of a skull.

Despite the menacing look, she smiles and says, "Welcome back, Cowboy."

01000100

"Fantom?" I mumble the name with an equal mix of disbelief and hopefulness.

She smirks. "Not exactly."

I open the social page attached to her avatar and see the name "Rayth."

"Fantom's a wanted criminal, yo. I can't be walkin' around usin' a flagged account." She taps her finger on my avatar's chest as she says, "And neither can you."

I look down at myself and see the avatar of a teenage boy. It's well-designed, but it isn't mine.

"I didn't exactly have time to clean your old account. I was a little busy trackin' you down and hackin' into your nanomachines. When I found out Ekko was still hangin' on to his son's old E-Womb, waitin' for their child license, well... It's sad, don't get me wrong, but it's good for you. The E-Womb was wiped when his son died, which made it easy for me to tag one of my ghost accounts onto the log-in functions."

I look down at my hand, waiting to see the flicker of bandwidth lag that Ekko suffered from, but nothing happens.

"I thought Old Mongolia's connections were toast. Outdated. But I'm not experiencing any lag."

"It isn't the infrastructure, yo," Fantom says. "It's DOTgov limitin' their access because they ain't providin' credits like the other countries. They're doin' the same with North America." She leans back with a smug grin. "But that ain't nothin'. If I can hack your nanomachines, you think a bandwidth cap is goin' to stop me?"

"I still don't understand how you could hack my nanomachines. No one can do that. I mean, how is that even possible?"

"I guess I'm just *that* good," she says, shrugging her shoulders and doing a poor job of looking humble.

"Being able to do something like that is... I mean, the privacy laws that you're breaking are—"

"Breakin' the law? I ain't exactly worried about that, Cowboy. DOTgov didn't protect us when we were stuck in that game, and they ain't fessin' up to the error either. So if I want to spend my time findin' the flaws in NextWorld, the stuff they ain't tellin' us about, then I'm figurin' there are worse ways to spend my time. Think about what I found. Hackin' nanomachines? I might be usin' it for good, but in the wrong hands? That could be seriously dangerous, yo."

"So that's what you've been doing since you logged-out? Fighting against DOTgov? Starting your own private revolution?"

I know I'm mocking her, but that's only to mask how impressed I am. She's always made me feel like less of a player. She's tough and cool and smart and confident and not impressed by me at all.

"DOTgov ain't evil, yo. They're just inept. I'm tryin' to pick up the slack."

"But how can you—"

"Look, Cowboy, we don't have time to catch up."

"Cyren," I manage to gasp her name. "How do you know the virus hasn't deleted her? It was consuming the world and—"

"I know. It deleted everything, yo. Includin' her. She hung on for a long time, but this morning it erased the last bit of code."

My heart skips a beat like it's going to give up on keeping me alive.

"But just because that virus deleted her, don't mean we can't still save her."

My words flutter, unable to gain traction as they leave my lips. "How... how..."

"When they were creatin' NextWorld, they put contingency plans in place in case there were any user errors that might delete somethin' important. They made sure to backup every piece of data marked for permanent deletion for twenty-four hours in a special domain."

She did it again. She gave me hope.

"A special domain? Where? What is it?"

Fantom leans back with a smile and says, "They call it the 'Trash Bin.' They'll store the game there until the timer runs out. We need to get in, cut her from the game, and paste her into NextWorld."

It sounds so simple when she says it, but I can't wrap my brain around how any of this could be possible. Although Fantom's hacking abilities have already proven that my version of possible is a bit outdated.

I start to accept the possibility of Cyren's face smiling back at me again when the truth threatens to destroy the fairy tale reunion I've been picturing in my mind.

"If the virus deleted her, then when we paste her into NextWorld it's going to be like a reboot," I start, my voice faltering, "Cyren won't..."

"No," Fantom says, looking away from me. "She won't remember anythin' stored in her Random Access Memory before the deletion. But whether she remembers you or not, she deserves a chance to live, yo."

My mind won't allow me to accept the information. It really *is* too late. No matter what, the Cyren I knew is gone. That unique collection of experiences and thoughts and emotions is lost. Forever.

Yet I can't let that stop me. I need to push away every selfish thought I'm having. I'm going to save the woman I love, even if it means she no longer loves me.

"I still don't understand how we can do this. How can we cut her from the game? NextWorld doesn't offer that ability in the average account options. Copying data is illegal."

Fantom shrugs one shoulder and gestures in the air, opening her inventory. She pulls a pair of scissors from the screen and holds them in front of me.

"It's a pretty basic hack, yo. I traded a friend of mine for a backdoor I opened in DOTxxx."

"DOTxxx? Why would a hacker want to—"

"Don't ask. With those types of people, it's always better not to ask."

I shake my head, trying to catch up to her plan. "Okay, but if we're going to use that program to cut her from the game and paste her into NextWorld, that means we still need to access the 'Trash Bin.'"

"First we'll need the location code for the game, which only DOTgov and the game company would have access to."

"But the game company is in DOTbiz."

"Now you're seein' the problem, yo. We can't get into DOTbiz unless we have an employee account."

"Can't you just hack us in?"

"Don't think I couldn't," she says, folding her arms over her chest and leaning back. "But DOTbiz has the best security that credits can buy. It's the best security that lots and lots of credits can buy. Even if I had a backdoor that could get us in, we don't have the time it would take for me to write up a new signal bounce to evade the domain's account tracker."

"What about Grael? If he can get us into the company database, then we could—"

"Not gonna happen. The government enlisted him to keep your game world runnin', but I think they're blockin' access to him or somethin'. There's no text, audio, or video-cast capability on his site in DOTbiz. We're going to have to get inside the domain to talk to him."

For a moment, I feel like it's over again. I lost. The rules are stacked against me. But I'm forgetting one thing. Now that I'm back in NextWorld, I'm no longer alone.

"You can enter DOTbiz with an employee account... or any family member of an employee. Right?"

"Sure. But your father works for DOTgov. That's not going to help us."

"I'm talking about Raev. Xen's partner. Her mother owns InfoLock."

Fantom smirks, knowing that we just found our loophole. "If she can get us inside, Grael can get us inside the company.

"Are you sure he'll help us? He wasn't exactly on board when we were in the game."

"Those are his programs, yo."

106

"The NPCs?"

"That whole world is his creation. No programmer is goin' to sit back while somethin', *anythin'*, deletes their work."

"Let's hope."

"Either way, we need to get movin'," she says as she walks away.

I jog to catch up to her and say, "Okay. Right," as I try to shift my brain back into gamer mode. I need to focus on the goal. I'm worrying too much about other people, trying to understand them. That's a hopeless battle for me. But saving Cyren? That I can do.

"If we need to find Raev, then we need to talk to Xen. We'll most likely find him in DOTgod."

Fantom lets out a snort. "Oh, I'm sure we will."

I open my inventory to see what I have for a vehicle. The screen appears in front of me, the empty white box glowing with blinding disappointment.

"Looks like I'm riding with you."

Fantom grins deviously and with a rather elaborate gesture of her hand, she opens what I assume is some kind of secret menu buried deep in her account. She selects something and an intricately designed rug unfurls in front of us. It lifts off the ground like a flying carpet, the tassels that surround it blowing in the wind.

"You have a flying vehicle? How did you come up with the credits to pay for—"

"Pay?" Fantom says with a laugh. "I don't pay, Cowboy. I'm a hacker."

"Wow," I whisper, my eyes darting back and forth. "This is *so* illegal."

"Get used to it, yo," she says as she climbs on to the front of the carpet.

I settle in next to her. With a tug on the edge of the material, the carpet lifts into the air. The air rushes past my head. The bandwidth speeds are incredible. I have no idea how she's bypassing the data cap, but I'm jealous. It's like she has all the cheat codes to the only game the entire world is playing.

When we exit DOTorg, the carpet swoops over DOTkid. Rainbows bend over the domain and brightly-colored mushrooms dot the rounded hills. Tiny avatars frolic in completely safe environments, sliding down candy canes and riding unicorns. Alphabet blocks construct pre-learning configurations, toppling over and bouncing like weightless feathers when one rather aggressive child decides to shove them. I remember fond moments with Xen in that place.

As we reach the center of the domain, I glance upward. Past the blue skies and fluffy white clouds, I see the metallic sheen of the spherical domain of DOTgov hanging in the sky, looking down upon all of NextWorld. Somewhere inside are the people responsible for my expulsion from NextWorld. The same people that are now hunting me, ready to throw me into a mind prison for my escape back into this world. The same people that are going to delete Cyren. The single, red flashing light stares back at me.

"Don't worry," Fantom says over her shoulder. "It can't see us. Hacker lesson number one."

I take her word for it and flip my middle finger into the air.

On the other side of DOTkid is the glowing domain of DOTgod. We dive through the pearlescent gates and fly a few feet above the heads of the religious pilgrims hiking down the golden path that splits the entire domain. It doesn't take us long to reach the entrance of a site that would be hard not to find impressive.

Through the golden gate is a golden castle piercing the sky, disappearing behind golden clouds that break apart to shine golden rays of light down upon the fields of golden wheat gently blowing in the wind. The men and women that stand in the fields appear to be unique humanoid avatars, but they are all dressed like Xen, with the same orange, monk-like robes.

"What is this place?"

Fantom throws her hands in the air and impersonates a preacher's boisterous, dramatic voice. "Welcome to the Mega-church of Metaversalism! Where the good and evil in all our hearts can find the one, true bliss!"

The followers near us cheer into the air when they hear her declaration, not understanding the sarcasm she meant. She laughs carelessly, but I cross my arms with a certain level of skepticism.

"Metaversalism? I've never heard of it. Why do you think Xen would attend a church like this?"

"Attend?" Fantom says, stepping off the flying carpet. "Cowboy, he doesn't attend this church. He leads it."

01000101

Fantom brazenly strolls through the crowds of Metaversalists, bumping shoulders and elbows as she makes her way to the front steps of the church. At first I excuse her brashness as I pass each avatar, but soon I'm distracted by the impressive sight of my best friend's accomplishment.

I'm having a hard time believing Xen leads his own church, no matter how fitting it is. There was a part of me that always believed, or maybe always hoped, that the rebellious side of Xen would break away from the dogmatic viewpoint of the church, not build an entirely new religion.

"I don't understand," I say, calling after Fantom as she confidently strides ahead of me. "What is this? What is Metaversalism?"

"You'd have to ask Xen if you want a real answer, yo. All I know is that a small sect of Omniversalists broke away from the church and formed this. It has somethin' to do with a disagreement over the ten thousand lessons of Omniversalism."

"Ten thousand? There are that many?"

The number seems ridiculous to me. No wonder he had a lesson for every situation.

"All the years you two were friends, I guess I figured you'd have learned a thing or two about his religion."

I slow my gait, a little ashamed to admit, "I mean, when I hear him talking, I'm usually waiting for him to stop."

There's an awkward silence as she glances over her shoulder at me, judging me and my friendship, but she doesn't say anything. She hops up the set of stairs that leads to the main doors and when she reaches the top of the steps, a golden avatar steps in front of her. When it holds out its hand to stop her, I notice that it's designed to look like nondescript version of Xen, lacking the detail of his avatar.

"I'm sorry," the avatar stopping us says, "but I can't allow you to enter this site until you register."

I step up to the avatar and say, "Tell Xen that his friend Arkade is—"

"Don't bother," Fantom says. "It's an NPC."

"How are we—"

"Not a problem."

Fantom swipes her hand in the air, opening that secret menu of hers. With a few selections, she pulls a key from her inventory that's crackling with electricity. With a single, strong thrust, she plunges the key into the NPC's chest, her arm disappearing all the way to the elbow. The Metaversalist avatars standing near us gasp in horror as the golden avatar writhes at the end of her arm. She twists the key inside and the NPC's face distorts, its eyes roll back in its head, and as it continues to repeat the registration protocol, its voice lowers and slows until the words are inaudible.

"There it is," Fantom says to herself, ripping her hand free.

The NPC stands up straight again, adjusting its eyes with a few blinks before noticing us.

"Welcome to the Mega-Church of Metaversalism," it says, motioning both hands toward the door and bowing at the waist. "May you find eternal bliss."

The grand, golden doors open with the sound of strumming harp strings.

"What was that?" I ask in a panicked whisper as I follow her through the entrance, glancing over my shoulder at the Metaversalists who are watching us with shocked looks.

"It's a simple registration key crack, yo." When she glances in my direction and sees my worried look, she rolls her eyes again and says, "You're goin' to have to man up and get used to this. I got a whole lot more illegal activities planned for us."

"I just... I mean, we did it right in front of all those avatars. Aren't you worried that—"

"Not really," she says so nonchalantly that I think she means it.

The entrance gives way to a long hall with a ceiling hundreds of feet above us. I notice words carved into the walls and eventually realize they are the lessons that Fantom was talking about.

"Light may produce shadows, but it can also destroy them," I read aloud as we pass. "No person is good or evil, they are the sum of their actions."

I continue to read the lessons as we travel through the hall, more to myself than anyone else, but after a while I can't take anymore.

"I don't understand how anyone can read this stuff and find guidance for their life. I mean, you could interpret this stuff to mean anything. People read this the way they want to read it. I bet if you asked a hundred Metaversalists what one of these lessons meant, you'd get a hundred different answers."

Fantom doesn't say anything. She just points at the last lesson on the wall before we step through another set of giant golden doors.

"Words mean nothing. Listen to your heart above all things. That is your truth."

I let out a frustrated shriek, "So they're actually admitting none of this matters? Why does Xen have all these lessons memorized if words mean nothing?"

"Maybe you should ask him," Fantom says.

Conducting a ceremony from a cross-legged position on a golden orb high above the entire congregation is Xen. His orange robes hang on his frail body and his eyes droop like he can barely see straight. He's manipulating music tracks on a large screen in front of him as the congregation sways back and forth below him. It looks more like a dance club than a church, but the sight of his avatar gives me a sense of comfort that only familiarity can achieve.

If I'm being honest, I'm drawn in for a moment. His music is commanding, booming against my chest, reverberating off the stained glass walls of the church with the pounding drum line and wobbly bass. There's a spiritual impressiveness to everything that makes me understand, for a split second, how someone could give up their logic and fall into the uplifting nature of something like this.

He's *good*.

"Xen," I mumble to myself.

Fantom swipes her hand in the air and checks some kind of display screen. "Well, apparently not. It's a prerecorded duplicate, yo. That's pretty strange. He doesn't even have a live session on the schedule."

"So where do we find him?"

She smiles as she looks over my shoulder and says, "I think *he* found *us*."

I spin around and see Xen and Raev descending a staircase. Raev doesn't notice us, but Xen stares at both of us with his mouth hanging open and his eyes wide. A group of Metaversalists swarm around him, asking him for blessings and answers to their questions. He pushes past the mob of followers and approaches us with a stumbling walk. As he gets closer, his walk turns into a wobbly jog, then a bouncing run. When he's a few feet from me, I realize his approach isn't aimed at me, but Fantom.

When he lifts her from the ground in a large hug, he says her name with excitement and disbelief whimpering together.

"Fantom?"

"The one and only, yo. Unless you count the mirror accounts I have running so the DgS can't monitor my real location."

He doesn't acknowledge what she says, instead turning toward me with a dazed look.

"Who's your friend?"

"Xen, it's me," I say.

His eyes blink once. Twice. There's a fog covering his mind that he tries to break through.

Fantom confirms, "It's Arkade."

His brain clicks with recognition and he falls toward me, his body collapsing into mine with an encompassing hug. I hold his skeletal body up as he cries into me, shaking with every whimper.

My shoulder muffles his mouth, but I hear him ask, "Is it really you? Tell me it's really you."

"It's really me."

He leans back from me without releasing his grip. "How are you... How is this...?"

"It's a long story," I say.

"Too long," Fantom says, stepping closer. "Right now, we're needin' to talk to your partner."

It takes Xen a moment. He sniffles his tears back inside and glances at Raev, who's still excusing Xen's behavior in front of the Metaversalists.

"Raev? What do you need to talk to her about?"

I look at Xen with as serious a face as my teenage boy avatar can summon and say, "We're going to save Cyren."

01000110

Xen and Raev's private chat room inside the mega-church is anything but cozy. The grandiose scale of the environment makes me feel both exposed and humble in comparison. We all float in the blackness of space, with stars twinkling light years away yet close enough to see every detail of their burning surface. As I float in awe of the vastness surrounding us, one of the stars implodes and devours its surroundings. It takes a few seconds for the implosion to consume the entire universe, only to cause an origin spark and explode into existence once again. Someone spent some time designing these graphics.

We're all standing on a small plot of land that houses a single tree, as if the universe ripped it from some earth that no longer exists. Roots protrude from the bottom of the loose soil.

"Cool" is all I manage to say, but no one hears me. Everyone is too busy trying to fit in their questions between everyone else's questions. We're all trying to catch up on years in a matter of minutes.

Before I explain my own story of my death trapping me in the log-out loop for so long and the virus attacking, Xen and Raev explain their experiences after graduation. They decided to take a pilgrimage through DOTgod, exploring the multitudes of other denominations and religions and philosophies. It was during these travels that they came across an old database from the early years of Omniversalism. No one had opened the files for decades. The files clearly stated there were originally only seven hundred and seventy-seven lessons of Omniversalism. Men and women trying to further their own agendas added the rest.

"There was a huge investor of the audio-cast," Xen explains, smiling and speaking with a slight chuckle as he pops a tiny red pill into his mouth. "He added the rules about never reading the lessons. You were only supposed to speak them."

Raev plops down against the tree and says, "After we knew where his credits were invested, it seemed kind of obvious why he wouldn't want people using text-casts to spread the word of Omniversalism."

"No doubt," Xen says with a wink toward Raev. "When we pieced together who made what new rule, the motivations and biases became quite clear. We couldn't continue teaching Omniversalism with a clear conscience."

This led them to create their own site within DOTgod where they could teach the original lessons, dubbed "The Sevens." They called it Metaversalism. Over time their venture turned into the mega-church we found them in.

Raev's mother still thinks that Xen has coerced her into some kind of cult that's taken over her life. She's still trying to bring her back into the DOTbiz domain to pursue a more secular path.

"It won't be a problem for me to get us into DOTbiz," she tells us, running her fingers across the thick grass. "I have an open invitation. But I'm guessing we don't want my mother tracking us, in which case we're going to have to wait until she logs-out."

"I don't know if we have that kind of time, yo," Fantom says.

"We don't have a choice. The possibility of her little lamb returning to the capitalist flock will always excite my mother." Raev chuckles at her own description and explains, "She has an automatic alert to let her know if I ever enter the domain."

Fantom looks anxious as she paces around the tree. I try to use logic and strategy to convince her.

"It's pointless to log-in to DOTbiz if we're going to get caught by some overbearing parent hovering around our accounts. We should wait."

Fantom doesn't look happy but she says, "This is *your* quest, Cowboy."

"Perhaps I'm mistaken, and if so, please correct me," Xen asks as he nonchalantly slides another pill into his mouth, "but won't the DgS be looking for Arkade? And if so, wouldn't they check up on any of the accounts associated with him? I'm not sure hanging out with the two players he was grouped with in *DangerWar 2* is the best idea."

"Why don't you leave the hackin' to me," Fantom says with a glare.

I hate to admit it, but, "He's got a point, Fantom. I think they would know that Xen is the first person I'd contact when I logged-in."

She lets out a long sigh, annoyed that she has to explain herself. "Look, you're on one of my old ghost accounts because you needed somethin' clean for the log-in. Once you were inside NextWorld, I rerouted your bandwidth so they can't track your E-Womb location. After that, hidin' your online activity is kiddie scripts. I'm doin' the same for all of us. We're invisible, yo."

"And the church?" Xen says, calm and smiling like his mind is floating high above any real sense of worry. "I can't have anyone in my congregation associated with any kind of illegal—"

Fantom holds up her hand to stop him. "As soon as we entered, I redirected any attempts at log-ins to an 'under construction' warning. The DgS can't send officers to check it out. As soon as we leave, I'll reconnect your traffic and no one will be any wiser."

"You hacked my church?"

It's the first time his smile falters.

Raev sets her hand on Xen's shoulder and says, "It'll be fine. We'll send out apologies to everyone for the inconvenience. They can survive a few hours without you."

"Sorry, Xen," I say, "but we need to do this. It's the only chance I have to save her."

Xen pops another pill into his mouth. His indulgence in the inebriating app is making me uncomfortable, but I don't have time to analyze it.

"Of course," Xen says, returning to his dazed, unconnected state.

After that, we bide our time. Raev constantly checks her parent's online status while we talk, sharing more stories from our time apart.

Fantom tells us about evading the DgS when she first logged-out from *DangerWar 2*, setting up her new account and bouncing around NextWorld for a few months. She soon realized her hopes for a career had become monumentally more difficult and would only serve to endanger her anonymity. She hung out more and more with the hackers in the DOTnet underground, meeting a few like-minded people that were trying to make NextWorld a better place, a place where people could be safe *and* free.

I find myself nodding along as Fantom's speech about the freedom of information turns into Raev and Xen comparing it to their own quest to expose the truth of Omniversalism's corruption. The idealism of all three of them is contagious. Why am I finding myself so swept away by everyone's grandeur? Is it because they're so secure with their place in life while I'm lost once again, displaced from my home? Am I just reaching for anything that will stop my fears from sweeping me away?

As their heated conversation continues, I try to make myself more comfortable. I open up my avatar design screen and start tweaking variables. I've felt awkward being inside someone else's form ever since I logged-in.

The first thing I do is change my height. I'm eighteen now, but even if I don't feel that old, I've never felt as young as this avatar makes me appear. I don't have time to design a whole bump-map for the flesh or do any kind of original shading, so I reluctantly choose something from the default choices. I feel better, even if I look like someone who spends all their time in DOTcom on a paid-advertisement account.

As my avatar changes, Fantom glances over at me and asks, "What are you doin'?"

I shrug my shoulders, trying to choose from the starter sets of t-shirts and pants that come with everyone's account. "Trying to feel like myself again."

She rolls her eyes. "I'm *not* travelin' around NextWorld with a basic avatar. Here." She swipes her hand toward me and my screen changes from a handful of choices and a limited color wheel to thousands of different items, clothing options, and body parts in a million different colors. "Pick somethin' better than... *that*. Please."

While I'm amazed at the offerings, I have to ask, "Did you steal these?"

She rolls her eyes again and I can't help wondering if she has that expression programmed as a loop on her avatar or if she reserves it especially for me.

"Steal? I don't *steal*. I'm not a thief."

"You're a hacker."

"I'm also a cracker, a phracker, and a sneaker. And I'm the girl that saved you from a life devoid of digital communications. Remember?"

"I'm just saying... these look expensive. Really expensive. And you said it yourself: you don't pay for anything."

"I don't pay for stuff because it's just data. Ones and zeroes. Like everythin' else in NextWorld."

"That's stealing. And I'm not comfortable using a stolen avatar."

"I might be breakin' some archaic, arbitrary law that I don't agree with, but even if I wanted to pay for those items, they aren't available in North America. We only have access to the most basic virtual items, just enough to get around and do our jobs. I don't exactly see that as fair. Do you?"

"No, but—"

"Well then, you can take your 'I'm better than you' attitude and shove it up your—"

"Some of these are your designs..." I say when I reach the menu labeled with her name. "These are better than the elite models they sell in NextWorld."

Raev looks over my shoulder at the screen in front of me. "Wow. Fantom. These are great! If you sold these on DOTcom, you'd make a fortune."

"No," Fantom says, her face darkening with her voice. "I wouldn't."

"A price you pay, I suppose, for using an illegal account," Xen says with a smile.

"Even if I had a clean account," Fantom barks back at Xen, "I'd still be forkin' over my North American reparations tax. We're only allowed to make a livin' wage. DOTgov takes the rest."

"That's still going on?" Raev asks. "I thought that stopped a long time ago."

Fantom mumbles to herself, "It's still goin' on because everyone who's not in North America forgets it's still goin' on."

Raev doesn't hear her, instead pointing at a necklace and saying, "That's beautiful."

"You're welcome to take anythin' you see. I don't care. It's just copies of copies of copies."

I scroll through the options, admiring Fantom's attention to detail in each piece. She's wasting her talent. I decide it's okay to take some copies as long as I stick to things she made. I'm not sure why that's more acceptable to me, but it is.

After I pick the perfect pair of jeans, I choose some dusty chaps, a shirt and vest combo, a weathered and beaten trench coat, and one perfectly bent cowboy hat. I slap a five o'clock shadow on the squarest jaw I can find, bulk up my chest and arms, and choose the most intimidating pair of eyes in the menu. I feel like myself again. I feel like Arkade.

"Is that better?" Fantom asks.

"Yeah. Thank you," I say. "Look, I'm sorry if I—"

"Don't worry about it," she says.

"No. Listen. I didn't mean to put down what you're doing or say that just because it's illegal it's not the right thing to do. You used some of these same hacks to save me. And now you're helping me save Cyren. Without you I'd be—"

"I *know*. You'd be a total loser, yo."

She laughs, and I join in, even though I don't find it funny... because I'm ashamed of how true it is. I'm not ashamed of being some social misfit like I assume she meant. I've been dealing with that my whole life. I'm ashamed of losing the game.

I lost. It's that simple. When the stakes were the highest, I failed at the one thing I thought I was good at. But Fantom gave me an extra life. She gave me a second chance and now all I can do is try to give Cyren the same thing.

It's a new quest in a new world and there's a new set of rules, but this time I'm going to win.

01000111

"She's out," Raev says, closing the screen she was using to monitor her mother's online status.

"Finally," Fantom says, wasting no time summoning her flying carpet and climbing aboard. "Just so you know, we can't be usin' this thing in DOTbiz. The security inside that domain is the strongest in NextWorld."

"You keep saying that. I have to admit, I'm surprised you're conceding that it's too strong for the great and powerful Fantom," I say with a smirk, taking maybe a little too much pleasure in finding the chink in her armor.

"You wish, Cowboy." Once we're all on the carpet, she yanks on the front and rockets into the sky, leaving DOTgod behind. "DOTbiz has the credits to do pretty much anythin' they want with their security. But even if I wanted to write a bypass algorithm for whatever measures they paid for, it'd be stupid to attract that much attention to the bandwidth usage this flyin' carpet needs. We're goin' to use somethin' a little more... standard."

Diving toward DOTbiz, a recognizable fear stretches out its cold fingers in my direction. I've always dreaded the fact that I'd probably end up here. There was no way I'd follow my father into DOTgov, and I knew if I didn't figure out some other plan, I'd be doomed to live out my days here in DOTbiz. Another corporate entity, paid to do some menial task because I'd be cheaper than buying an NPC.

Even if I was "lucky" enough to work for some game company, creating the very thing that I loved, I knew I'd become nothing more than a piece of a machine, with no real contributing power to the overall product. Another zero in a sea of binary.

The entrance to DOTbiz looks so generically uninspired, I'm immediately bored. There's a minimalist style to everything. Gray monotone colors cover the soft edges of every wall. Ferns and philodendrons spot the open areas, perfectly green and spaced an appropriate distance apart. Someone designed everything to neutralize emotion and stamp out individual thought. I'm ready to fall into a dazed trance when I remind myself what's waiting on the other side of the arched gates.

When we land, Fantom summons a different vehicle from her inventory that can accommodate multiple avatars. It's a brown, four-door sedan that looks like every other vehicle entering the domain. I'm about to complain when I realize that it's the perfect way to blend in with the monotony.

"I'm drivin'," Fantom says as she climbs into the driver's seat.

I climb in the passenger side and look over the seat at Xen and Raev in the back. "This is going to work. Right?"

"Course it's goin' to work," Fantom says, answering for them.

"I haven't stepped foot in here since a job shadow I did for my DOTedu senior class project," Raev says. "I promised myself I'd never come back..."

"We won't be here long," Xen says, popping a pill and peeking out his window like he's on a safari in a foreign land.

I look back and forth at them both, watching them clasping hands and smiling, offering each other their strength.

They were safe before I showed up. They were in a place that didn't threaten their viewpoints. There was no risk of upsetting everything they accomplished. Their life protected them. They had achieved their goal. They were able to relax in the reward together.

Cyren and I used to have that.

"Thank you for doing this," I say to Raev. "I know that I already put Xen in danger once. Now here I am, doing it again."

Raev reaches forward and puts her hand on my arm. "Xen's a big boy. He can make his own decisions. Besides, Metaversalism teaches us that the more we bleed, the thicker the scar will be that protects us."

I'm about to call her out on how little sense that lesson makes to me, but I stop myself.

"I want you to know how much I appreciate everything you're doing. I promise I'll get you two back to your church as soon as I can."

"As long as you promise to visit us more often," Xen says with a smile.

"Of course."

"And maybe attend a service or two while you're there?"

"We're next," Fantom says as our car rolls through the archway.

I turn around in my seat, thankful for the rescue from Xen's request. There's a beep in my ear, then a chime of approval. The same screen pops up in front of each of our faces, acknowledging our companion's family-approved DOTbiz account. It contains a long, legal document listing what we can and can't do, how far away from Raev we're able to be at any given time inside the domain, and the names of prohibited streets. We all press the accept button without reading it and our car is thrust into DOTbiz.

The windowless skyscrapers of the domain all look exactly the same. There is no commercialization or marketing allowed here, just utilitarian storage space. Each office structure stretches toward a sky that isn't sunny or cloudy. There's no contrast. The road is the same color as the sidewalk which is the same color as the buildings that happen to be the same, monotone gray as the sky. A deep, choking depression hovers over the domain like a cloud of smog. We slide through the streets, passing company cars that offer a minimal amount of bandwidth. The employees inside hang their heads low as they make the slow crawl to whatever employer deemed them useful enough to pay.

"And to think, you had to give up all this to become a hacker," I say with a smirk.

"I should have had a choice," Fantom says, her jaw firmly clenched.

I can tell my joke made her angry, but I don't understand why. She has an inventory of items, she doesn't have to pay for a thing, she's got unlimited bandwidth, and DOTgov barely knows she exists. If that isn't freedom, I don't know what is.

The streets of DOTbiz roll under our car, each intersection passing us like clockwork, every block the exact same size and shape. The designers meant for the uniformity of everything to bring a sense of fairness and equality to the domain, giving every business a fair advantage, but the idea is ludicrous. As soon as they unleash their products into DOTcom, the company with the most money for marketing always comes out on top.

The monotone landscape bores me into submission. I'm woken from the glaze covering my eyes when Fantom says, "It's just ahead."

The mapping software built into the vehicle directed her here, but to the rest of us, it's just another building with one unmarked door on the front.

As we step out of the sedan, it disappears back in to Fantom's inventory. There's a moment of shared hesitation before we enter the building, but I push past it, knowing that I'm getting closer to Cyren with every step I take. I open the door and step into a white room. A turret drops down from the ceiling and my gamer instincts force me to duck and roll to the side. The turret stays locked on to me, but instead of spitting out bullets, it scans my body.

"You do not have permission to enter."

I look over my shoulder as the rest of the group enters. The turret spins, scans each one, and repeats the same phrase.

"I hope you have a way to hack this," I say to Fantom.

She rolls her eyes at me and says to the turret, "We're requestin' guest passes to visit employee name: Grael."

The turret blinks as it rests in silence. I glance at Raev and Xen who look extraordinarily nervous. They look to me, hoping that I have something to offer them in the way of assurances. I divert my eyes.

"Guest access granted for one hour," the turret says before lifting back into the ceiling.

Fantom smiles back at us as the door on the opposite side of the room opens. Xen and Raev step forward to follow her through. I slip past everyone, unable to slow myself. I'm afraid of what will happen if I stop for too long. I have to keep moving, toward my goal, toward Cyren.

01001000

Shoulder-high cubicle walls intersect each other, creating a well-organized maze that stretches into the infinite distance. There are no workstations inside the cubicles and no employees doing any actual work.

With a few selections in my social menu screen I manage to find Grael's avatar in the center of the endless room. I highlight his location for everyone and make my way down corridor after corridor of beige cubes. A single chair sits inside each one, but the walls are bare. It's an empty room full of tinier empty rooms. It's what I imagined DOTbiz to look like in my nightmares.

When I find the middle of the office, I see Grael leaning back in his chair, staring at the ceiling. He looks the same, with his red dreadlocks pulled behind his head, but his bulletproof vest and gas mask are missing. He's wearing a plain gray suit coat, his tie loosely hanging around his neck. Other than a single screen floating in front of him, his cubicle is empty.

He seemed so powerful to me inside the game. I found him intimidating, lording his higher Level over me. Now he looks dull. Weak.

"Grael?" Xen says as he touches his shoulder.

Grael jerks and looks at us, rubbing his thumbs into his eyes. "I should have known *you'd* come here."

"What are you doing?" I ask, my eyes scanning the emptiness around him.

"Waiting."

We all exchange nervous glances, unsure of his state of mind.

"What are you waitin' for, yo?" Fantom asks.

He shrugs his shoulders. "I'm waiting. I'm waiting until I can't wait any longer." He leans back in his chair again and spins, staring up at the ceiling as it twirls above him. He speaks fast, his mouth barely keeping up with the chaos of his thoughts.

"Do you know that they forced me to work here? It was the only place I could log-in to. This domain. This site. This company. Just me. In this room. All day. Every day. They meant it as some kind of punishment. But do you want to know a secret?"

He stops spinning and leans forward, staring at us with a devious smile stretching from ear to ear.

"I didn't want to be anywhere else." He opens his arms wide as if he's presenting the room to us. "This is where I belong. In my home, with my children."

"Your 'children?'" Raev asks, waiting for us to admit that Grael seems as crazy to us as he does to her.

"He's talkin' about the NPCs," Fantom says, crossing her arms. "Aren't you?"

Grael looks at me and says, "You were right all along, kid. Once I was outside the game world and I could look at the code, I saw how much it had changed from what I originally wrote." Grael's voice is shaking with excitement. "They were learning. They were conscious. They were self-aware. All of them."

He stands up and rushes toward me. I flinch, thinking it's some kind of attack, but the non-PvP area logo is flashing in my view. His face is inches from mine, his eyes wild with excitement.

"I wouldn't have trusted anyone else to protect them. I *had* to do it myself. It was an honor. A privilege. I got to witness them making history."

He pulls away from me, throwing his hand into the air as he continues his tirade.

"I tried to tell them! I tried to show everyone what I had created. But they wouldn't listen. They thought I was crazy."

He starts laughing. It's a cackling, high-pitched laugh, like a young boy trying to mask crying.

"They were acting like I acted when you tried to convince me that my game was alive."

"It's okay," I say, trying to calm him down, but he twirls around and puts himself in my face again.

"No, it's not," he mumbles. "It's not okay. I failed. I failed to protect them. My children. Maybe if NextWorld had known the truth, maybe they would have done more. Maybe they would have helped me."

He turns to Fantom and says, "I don't know how the virus got in. We had so much of the game locked down. No connection. No patches. The firewall just dropped away. I've looked at the data over and over. I don't know what I did wrong."

Fantom says nothing. There's a long pause as I hesitate to reply.

"You didn't do anything wrong," I say, almost unable to admit the truth. "It was my fault."

Everyone flashes a stunned look in my direction.

"I died. I was being stupid, going on an adventure that I didn't need to go on. All because I was bored. Because I wanted to keep playing. Because... I don't know. The civilians took down the firewall so they could reroute my spawn point. They did it to save me... and they ended up dooming themselves in the process."

Fantom shakes her head. "You both need to stop blamin' yourselves. That virus wasn't some malware floatin' around NextWorld. It was an intentional attack, yo."

"Who would do that?" Xen asks.

"I don't know," I say with both hands curled into fists. "But when I find out, they're going to pay."

"The other question is *why* would someone do that," Raev asks. "Why would someone want to destroy something you worked so hard to create?"

"I didn't create them," Grael says, his body losing its energy as he sits back down in his cubicle. "They were a fluke. A mistake. I made an accidental connection. The NPCs I designed should never have been capable of the things they were doing. I thought maybe with more time I could understand..."

"What if I told you there was still time," Fantom says.

I can't help smiling when Grael perks up. I know the look in his eyes. That renewed sense of hope. The chance to gain back everything he's lost.

"When was the game deleted?" Fantom asks. "When did the virus delete the last line of code?"

Grael looks confused as he mumbles, "The virus deleted the last line of code this morning."

"I need to know the *exact* time."

Grael wipes his mouth with the back of his hand and opens a screen in front of him, accessing the game company records.

"It was 0818, NextWorld time."

Fantom opens her own screen, swiping through menus. With a few flicks of her wrist, she shares a timer with all of us that appears in the corner of our views. It's counting down from just under eighteen hours.

"Open your workstation," Fantom says as she pulls up a chair next to Grael in his cubicle. "We've got to find the location code for the game world data or we'll be wanderin' around the Trash Bin forever, yo."

"The Trash Bin?"

For once, Fantom rolls her eyes at someone other than me. As search screens open in front of her, she says, "Do your best to keep up."

01001001

Raev and Xen join me in a nearby cubicle. I'm trying to catch up to my emotions without imploding from the pressure. Xen sits down across from me on the floor with that stupid grin on his face. It's driving me crazy.

"What?"

He tilts his head to the side and says, "I'm just... happy to see you, Kade. You were trapped in that log-out loop for so long, you know? I tried to keep my hope that maybe Cyren could convince the civilian NPCs to reinstate the log-out, but after a while I had to accept the fact that they weren't going to sacrifice themselves just to let you go. Which meant the only hope in seeing you again would be for DOTgov to do a cold reboot of your E-Womb. The idea that they would fry your nanomachines was just too much for me."

Raev reaches out and touches Xen as she says, "I think it reminded him of his own time stuck in the loop."

Xen pops another pill and says, "I found ways to deal with it."

"The NPCs chose to release me when their world was gone, when there was... nothing left to fight for." I suck in a deep breath, forcing myself to push forward. "But they were wrong. There *was* something left to fight for. Cyren was still alive. We could have survived. We could have..."

I lose my words. I'm not sure whether I'm sad, or angry, or maybe something else entirely. It gets all mixed up inside me. I need a villain, an enemy, something to blame, something to fight. I wish I could just shoot something.

"You can't just survive," Raev says calmly, twisting her ribbon hair around one finger. "You need to live. *Truly* live."

"When we first became partners, I thought that I had achieved everything I needed in life," Xen says, smiling at Raev. "I stopped frequenting DOTsoc. I stopped going to clubs and concerts. I wanted to spend all my time meditating in DOTgod with Raev. I thought that was all I needed." He touches her face. "She was the one that showed me the error in my ways. She was the one that showed me the wastefulness in a life lived solitary, denying myself all the pleasures that NextWorld has to offer."

He runs his fingers across his mouth and I see a red pill disappear between his lips.

"It's about balance," Raev says, looking deep into Xen's eyes, yet talking to me. "Moderation in either direction can bring you a lot of pleasure, just like falling to either side can cause a lot of pain."

"Are you preaching to me right now?"

Xen chuckles. "Don't bother, Raev. I gave up trying to convert Kade when he was ten."

I think again about what Raev said about moderation, and when Xen pops yet another red pill, I wonder if maybe she was preaching to him. The thought fades away as I'm consumed again by my own issues.

"I don't think I've really accepted what's happened. I don't think I've had time to stop and consider everything. Cyren chose her death so that I could live. And now, even if I save her, she won't remember me."

"What she did wasn't a choice. Not to her," Raev says. "She would have done anything to save you."

"She loved you, Kade. You'd have done the same thing for her."

"Of course I would have!" I blurt out, hearing my own argument. I'm trying to argue with two people that I agree with for no other reason than my own frustration with having nothing else to lash out at.

They're doing nothing but sacrificing for me. They're putting themselves at risk to help me save the woman I love. Because *they* love me.

"I'm sorry," I mumble.

"Kade, it's okay. We just—"

"No. Listen to me." I rub my face, collecting my emotions and setting them in the appropriate containers in my mind. "Thank you. Both of you. I still need to remind myself now and then that sometimes I need help. Sometimes I need a group."

"I'm your best friend, Kade. I'm never leaving your group."

"And I'm his partner," Raev says with a smile. "So I guess you're stuck with me, too."

I shake my head, a smile breaking across my face. "Someday, I hope I can repay you."

I start by asking them questions about Metaversalism. And I listen. I *really* listen. I don't give them any snide replies to the lessons they adhere to. I don't fade out when Xen's slurred speech trails off on tangents that aren't connected to the point he was trying to make. I don't point out the contradictions in their translations of the seven hundred and seventy-seven lessons. I listen to them and do my very best to understand them. Because they are my friends.

"We got it, yo," Fantom says, standing up triumphantly from the cubicle next to us and swiping her screen shut. She turns to Grael and says, "Share the location code with my account and I'll encrypt it with—"

"On one condition," he says, afraid to make eye contact with her.

"Condition?" I ask defensively, standing up and approaching him with my hands balled into fists.

He holds up a hand to stop me. "You're here to save Cyren. That's good. I get it. But there's a whole game world of NPCs in there. You need to save all of them."

I look at Fantom and she nods. "The program can cut them all out. It shouldn't be a problem, yo."

"Fine," I say. "They all deserve to live. We'll cut them from the game and paste them into NextWorld so they can—"

"It's not that simple," he barks at me before calming himself down. "DOTgov wants to destroy them because they don't know how to control them. Their processing power could multiply with every second we allow them to exist in NextWorld. They could consume every bit of data, increasing their intelligence exponentially. They could become... I don't know. I have no idea what they might be capable of if they work together in the vastness of the network. But if we let them loose in NextWorld, the DgS could track them down and delete them again."

"So... what? What do you want me to do with them?"

Grael looks up at me and says, "I need to look at their code. I think I have a way to stop DOTgov from being able to delete them, but I need more time."

I look to Fantom, hoping for her opinion, but she shrugs her shoulders and says, "Your call, Cowboy."

I don't want to decide. I want to save Cyren.

"Fine. As long as I can free Cyren, you can have the others."

"Thank you. I—" Grael stops and steps backward to swipe a pop-up screen away from his view.

When Fantom does the same thing, she yells, "We have to go. Now!"

"What is it?" I ask.

Before they can explain, a pop-up screen appears in front of me, alerting me that our guest pass is about to expire.

Fantom runs for the door, yelling over her shoulder, "The trespass will alert the DgS."

I look back at Grael.

He swipes his hand, sharing the location code of the game and pointing toward the exit. "Just go! Save them, Arkade. Save them *all*."

I jog after Fantom, still not sure of what is happening. "I thought you were hiding our accounts?"

She turns around, screaming at me. "I am! Nothin' would have flagged our accounts as long as we didn't do anythin' abnormal inside the domain."

"How about we stop arguing and get out of the domain?" Xen says, his pills keeping him more calm than any of us.

We burst through the exit of the office, out on to the street, but we're stopped in our tracks when ten DgS officers teleport on to the pavement. They're furiously swiping their hands through the air, checking scanners and readouts on our accounts, trying to break through Fantom's blocks.

"They're going to be able to read Raev's account. I couldn't put the same ghosting patterns on her as us because she's still connected to her mother's account. As soon as they see that connection..."

"I'm sticking with my original plan," Xen says, backing away from them. "The one where we get out of this domain."

"They locked down the domain," Fantom says in a hushed tone. "I'm going need time to break us out."

"What do we do in the mean time?" Raev asks, looking excited by the danger.

Fantom grinds her teeth together, looking up and down the street before she answers. "We run."

01001010

The DgS officers step forward as Fantom opens up her inventory and unfurls her carpet in front of us so that it hovers a foot off the ground.

"Get on!" she screams as the DgS officers run toward us.

We all step on to the material as it lifts from the ground, leaving the officers staring at us from the street below. I'm about to take in a breath of relief when Xen says with a passing interest, "I think they're chasing us."

I look behind us and see the DgS officers lift off the ground, rocketing into the sky without any vehicle.

"They're tracin' our signal," Fantom says before banking to the left as two more officers teleport into the sky in front of us. "And they're doin' a good job, yo."

Raev leans down next to her and says with an odd calm, "Then you have to do a better job."

"I'm tryin'," Fantom says, diving between two monotone buildings before turning right and sliding down an alleyway. "But I told you, DOTbiz has the most elaborate security in NextWorld, because they can afford to have the most elaborate security in NextWorld. This ain't gonna be easy, yo."

"Did you need me to do anything?" Xen says, dropping a handful of pills as we bank around five more officers appearing in front of us, trying to block the alleyway.

"Stop talkin'!" Fantom screams, yanking the rug upward, climbing toward the sky above DOTbiz.

I watch her control the rug with one hand while trying to maneuver through her secret menu screens with the other. I crouch down next to her and grab on to the rug. She glares at me for a second before I say very simply, "I'll drive. You hack."

She hesitates, not wanting to give up control of the rug. Three more officers teleport in front of us. They reach out to grab us as we pass, missing us by a few inches.

"I don't care who does what," Raev yells. "Just get us out of here!"

Fantom turns away from the front of the rug and swipes through her screens with both hands. "We won't be able to leave the domain until I can hide Raev's account, bypass the lockdown security, and activate a bug-out algorithm." She ducks as another officer appears and swipes his hand at her. "They have to touch us in order to do anythin' to our accounts, so just stay away from them and give me time!"

Officers appear all around us, teleporting in with flashes of light, like tiny explosions across the sky. Changing the direction of our bandwidth to dodge around them isn't unlike playing a game. I watch the arrangement of the appearances and try to guess where they'll appear next, then I aim us somewhere else. It takes constant calculating, but when my gamer brain clicks into the pattern, I don't see anything else. Like tunnel vision, the rest of the domain disappears and all I see is our trajectory.

I'm so lost in operating the flying carpet, soaring back and forth, doubling back through alleyways and skimming across rooftops, that I'm not sure how much time passes before Fantom yells, "Got it!"

She points at a hole in the edge of the domain, like an opening torn in the sky. I pull up on the carpet, then bank to the left, shooting directly toward the exit. We blast through the lockdown that surrounds the domain and the hole seals behind us. As we zoom over the super-highway that connects the domains of NextWorld, Fantom grabs a hold of the carpet again.

I relinquish control back to her and ask, "Why aren't they following us out here?"

"They are. At least, they think they are," she says with a wink. "Once they find 'us' they'll realize they've been tracking a family of accounts from Old India."

"Did they complete their scan?"

Fantom looks at me like what I'm asking is ludicrous. "What do you think I am? Of course they didn't scan us. We're clean, yo."

I turn around and face Raev and Xen. "I can't thank you enough. I'm sorry it came so close, but we can bring you back to DOTgod now. The DgS will never know you helped me."

Xen opens his mouth to accept my thanks, but Raev cuts him off.

"You've got to be joking. You're going to bring us home just when things are getting interesting?"

"You don't have to—"

"But we're going to," she says, looking away from me to end the conversation.

Fantom glances at me and I shrug my shoulders in response, settling back into my spot next to her. She pushes down on the carpet and we dive toward the edge of the super-highway. We skim across the last lane and head straight for a large tree trunk sitting on a hill. As we get closer, the top of the tree trunk pops open. The carpet dives into the opening and we drop into a sewer-like tunnel covered in tubes, cords, and wires. The carpet comes to a stop and disappears from underneath us.

"Welcome to DOTnet, yo," Fantom says as she falls against the brick wall, exhausted.

I check my location screen and it confirms what she's saying, but I still don't fully believe it.

"This doesn't look like DOTnet."

I've been to the domain once before to upload my information for the student voucher program because something went wrong and DOTedu lost my files. The domain looked like a giant circuit board, with buildings like electrical components and passageways etched from copper sheets. I got lost three times even though I was using the domain's mapping program. Everyone who worked there acted like every one of my problems was my own fault. No one visits DOTnet unless it's absolutely necessary. Today definitely qualifies.

"We're under the domain," Fantom says, pointing at the ceiling. "These tunnels are under *all* of the domains. DOTnet connects all of NextWorld. It's the infrastructure that sends the bits and pieces travelin' through *here* before they're goin' up *there*." She grins to herself and adds, "Which is why my people like it so much."

"Your people?" Xen asks.

"Hackers, yo. We use these tunnels to access back doors, listen in on casts, or slip our own command lines into all the noise that's runnin' through here."

My timer clicks down, each number rolling over to signify the loss of another second, another minute, another hour. Sixteen hours left. Sixteen hours until I lose everything. Sixteen hours to save her.

"Is this how we're going to enter the Trash Bin?" I ask, trying to push everyone closer to our goal. "Do we hack into one of these tubes and—"

"Not so fast, Cowboy." Fantom turns and heads deeper into the network of sewers. "I said I knew about the Trash Bin. I never said I knew how to get in."

"You don't know *how* to get in?" My words shriek, my voice breaks, and I sound like a whiny kid again.

"No," she says carelessly, "but I know someone who does."

"Another hacker?" Raev asks, and I'm surprised by how excited she sounds by the prospect.

"You could say that. He leads one of the most elite groups down here. Sektor. They're snoopin' and sniffin' every corner of NextWorld, all in the name of information freedom. They'd prefer it if you called them hacktivists, yo."

"So where do we find this 'hacktivist'?"

She runs her hands down her pigtails and throws them out to the sides. "We can't just *find* him."

"Great," I say with an exasperated sigh, taking my cowboy hat off and running my fingers through my own hair.

"If we can't find him...?" Raev asks, unsure how to end her question.

"He'll find us, yo. We just need to make ourselves noticeable."

"I thought that was dangerous," Xen says, rubbing his eyes as if he's trying to look past his own confusion. "Didn't you say we needed to stay hidden?"

"Down here, hackers have a few safe havens, places where DOTgov can't snoop around. We go to one of those places and we wait."

"Are you sure we can trust him?" I ask, worried about the casualness of the plan, not to mention relying on yet another person.

"Nope. In fact, the one time I *did* trust him, he ended up breakin' off our partnership for another girl."

01001011

"You're telling me that the hacker we're trying to find used to be your partner?" Raev asks.

"Yeah," Fantom says as she continues down the underground passage.

Xen catches up to her and asks, "Was this the one that broke up with you right before you played *DangerWar 2*?"

"Yup. Same one, yo."

Xen sets his hand on Fantom's shoulder. "Are you sure you want to ask him for help? I can see the pain in your eyes, no matter how much you try to hide it."

Fantom laughs. "Ain't no pain, yo."

Xen tilts his head as if he's waiting for Fantom to tell him the truth.

Fantom laughs again. "What? I'm serious. I'm glad I'm done with his pretentious nonsense. He was always correctin' me and tellin' me how he wants me to be a better me and tryin' to school me on the ways of NextWorld. Forget that. I'm blazin' my own trail, yo."

"If you say so," Xen says, like he knows there's more to it than she's letting on.

"Not every woman needs a partner," Raev says, "no matter what DOTgov or DOTgod tries to tell you."

Xen stops as the two girls keep walking together. "Hey," he calls out after them, jogging to catch up. "I wasn't trying to say... I didn't mean... I was just trying to show some sympathy."

When they both laugh and keep walking, Xen turns to me and asks, "What just happened?"

I shrug. "You don't seriously think I would have any clue, do you?"

He shakes his head, visibly turning over the interaction in his mind, trying to make sense of it all. He digs into the inventory where he keeps his pills, but he finds an empty screen.

We don't travel far when Fantom stops. I'm confused by our destination. There are no discernible markings. It looks indistinguishable from the rest of the tunnels.

Fantom looks at one of the brick walls, leaning in close to search for a tiny detail. When she finds what she's looking for, she places her hand on one of the bricks and pushes. The brick sinks in, then slides back into place. The entire wall releases a cloud of dust as it breaks free and shifts to the side.

"This way," Fantom says, stepping through the secret entrance.

On the other side of the doorway is a small room with red velvet covering every surface. Chairs line one wall and a concierge stands behind a desk, marking things down in a large book. On the far side of the room is an elevator door.

Fantom saunters through the room, nods at the man behind the desk, and steps up to the elevator door. There's no call button or any apparent way to open the door.

"Now what?" I ask.

"Patience," she says. "You didn't think it would be that easy to get into this place, did you?"

"This is so cool," Raev says. Seeing the surprised look on Xen's face, she defensively says, "What? I can't help it. I've never done anything illegal before."

The concierge clears his throat.

Fantom whispers over her shoulder, "Would you play it cool, yo? We ain't doin' nothin' illegal. The people who run this site? That's another story. But we're just visitin'. So try to act like you belong. Okay?"

Raev nods her head.

Fantom places her hand on the elevator door for five seconds, then forms a fist and knocks five times. There's a pause before five more knocks. She presses both palms against the door. The door completely vanishes and we can see the interior of the elevator, with wood paneled walls and a flickering light above. She motions for us to step in. Once we do, the door reappears and we hear a chime before the elevator drops out from under us. I have a quick flashback to my escape from the tower as we plummet to the bottom of wherever we are. I let out a short yelp right before the elevator slows to a stop. There's another chime. Xen and Raev look at me with surprise, but Fantom ignores my outburst and presses both of her palms on the doors again.

The elevator doors disappear, and we see a long white hallway extending into the distance. Every ten feet there is another hallway crossing it. Fantom walks boldly through the maze of intersections, turning at what appears to be random intervals. I'm lost within seconds. Left, left, right, left, straight, right. At one point she stops, spins three times to the left, and starts walking back the way we came. I'm ready to question her, to ask what nonsense she's leading us into, but she's leading us with an air of confidence that calms my apprehension.

After a few minutes of traversing the maze, she turns a corner and we're met with a doorway made of the same red velvet as the room with the elevator. Fantom flashes one last grin before she pushes open the door.

"Welcome to Club L33T, yo."

Strange music pumps through the dark, bar-like interior, which is only lit by screens that cover the walls. Each screen is displaying something different: statistical data on bandwidth usage, open and closed ports around NextWorld, bird's eye views of games in DOTfun, underground auction sites, news-casts, and hacked point-of-views from different user's accounts. The main area of the bar is scattered with tables that have shadowy figures hunched over them. Some are speaking to each other in whispers, while others are consumed by whatever is happening on their own private screens. Another gathering of avatars are placing bets on a DOTfun racing game that they're all watching on the wall. More groups stand around the actual bar, ordering strange inebriating downloads. Every person stops for a second to take note of us entering before returning to whatever they were doing before we stepped in.

I try not to make eye-contact as I follow Fantom through the crowd. She strides confidently past the cyborgs and robots next to the jukebox before sliding into a table in the corner, placing herself with her back to the wall. Xen, Raev, and I slide in next to her. We all hunch over the table like everyone else, leaning in close to speak in whispers.

Xen looks confused, like he's trying to think of a word that's escaping him. He keeps tilting his head from side to side until he asks, "What is this music? I've never heard anything like it before."

Fantom shrugs her shoulder and says, "That's because DOTgov ain't gonna authorize it, yo. Independent pirate bands. You won't hear this stuff on the audio-casts."

The singer is shouting over the squawking and chirping digital sounds, and it's apparent why DOTgov's Department of Art would never authorize it.

"We ain't gotta listen to President Chang! It's time for us to string 'im up and let 'im hang!"

Xen swipes his hand and opens the club's menu screen, his eyes growing with excitement as he proclaims, "They have Dizzy Fizz apps!"

Raev gently grabs Xen's hand before he's able to order them. "Those can be quite strong."

"I know!" he says with a giddiness that doesn't match her apprehension. "I dropped the last of my Simmer Pills when we were flying around DOTbiz."

Raev considers saying more before reluctantly taking her hand off his. He orders the tabs of blue gel without hesitation.

I slide closer to Fantom.

"Do you see him?" I ask out of the corner of my mouth as I gaze around the bar, wondering what type of person Fantom would date.

"No. But he ain't choosin' to be visible."

"What does that mean?"

She rolls her eyes, swipes her hand in the air, and vanishes. I flinch, not expecting the abrupt disappearance. I flinch again when she reappears.

"Most avatars use their eyes to see NextWorld," she says. "That's why most avatars are easy to trick. You can't rely on your vision."

"So, what? I'm supposed to smell you?"

Her eyes flash in my direction. "You put your nose anywhere near me and you'll be regrettin' it."

"Then maybe you could enlighten me as to how we find an invisible hacker."

She lets out a sigh and leans forward with that bored look in her eyes, but I know better. She's loving this. She gets to lord her superior knowledge over me and prove how much smarter she is than me. I wonder how much of this she had to put up with when she was learning from other hackers.

"The problem is, people are treatin' NextWorld like it's real. People are doin' the same stuff people were doin' in the real world, only they're doin' it in here. It's like it's a replacement or somethin'. They don't realize it's somethin' completely new."

She's waving her hands around, getting more passionate about what she's saying. "This place is just information. Data. Ones and zeroes. All of it." She taps on the wooden table. "There's no difference between you and this table. Between the music you're hearin' and the screen you're watchin' or the food you're tastin' or the game you're playin' or... whatever. It's all the same. It's all connected. Seein' your avatar ain't no different than hackin' your avatar. As long as you know what you're doin', yo."

She sits up straight and throws her hands out, showing off her kimono. "When you see me, you're turnin' my ones and zeroes into this fabulous lookin' avatar I designed. When I see you, I'm usin' those ones and zeroes a little more... *creatively*."

She actually piques my interest. I don't like the fact that there's a whole side to NextWorld that I don't use. Suddenly I need to know everything about hacking, but before I can ask another question, Fantom goes stiff when she glances across the club.

I follow her gaze and see three avatars walking toward us. Their bodies are completely wrapped in chains, with three-foot-high mohawks protruding from the top and glowing eyes peering out between the metal links.

"Who are they?" I whisper.

She clenches her teeth and says, "Trouble."

01001100

The chain-covered avatar standing in front of his two friends says, "I'm needin' some malware."

Fantom sits there, not saying a word.

He keeps talking. "Nothin' too big, yo. Just a graphics hack so I can deface a DOTorg site that banned me."

His friends laugh and high-five each other.

Fantom doesn't react.

I gesture with my hand to open the social screens for the three men, but they've blocked access.

"Hey," the leader says, pressing his chain-wrapped finger into the table, "I said I'm needin' malware. And I know you're holdin'."

"I don't sell malware," Fantom says through her teeth.

"Yeah. I know. I heard you do it for free, yo. Why do you think I'm talking to you?"

"I don't write malware. But even if I did, I wouldn't be givin' you anythin'."

The leader stands up straight, surprised by her reply. He looks over his shoulder at his two friends. They just shrug at him in reply. He places both of his hands on our table and leans in.

"Crymsin and KaosKing told me you were tight sometimes." He licks his lips. "What's it gonna take for me to open you up?"

Xen and Raev exchange worried looks. Xen nervously slides a Dizzy Fizz between his lips.

I look at Fantom.

Fantom disappears.

For a split second I think she's left us. I think she's decided we're too much trouble and she went invisible to sneak out some back entrance. But before anyone can react, she reappears on the table, slamming a sword into the chain-covered avatar's hand. He lets out a scream. When the other two avatars step back, she yanks the sword out from the table and slashes it through the air in one fluid motion. A chain-covered head with a mohawk goes rolling across the floor. A second later the entire avatar disappears. His two friends reach into their inventories and pull out long chains, which they swing in circles as they spread out, trying to flank Fantom.

Fantom doesn't hesitate.

She lunges for the one on the right, stabbing the end of her sword through his chest. His avatar disappears. The other one swings his chain at her but she ducks underneath and chops him off at the knees. He tumbles to the floor where she decapitates him with another swing. His avatar disappears. She slides her sword behind her back, placing it into some secret inventory and blinks out of view before reappearing back in her seat. The whole battle only takes a few seconds.

Xen, Raev, and I are still sitting in the same positions, our mouths hanging open. The rest of the bar doesn't react, as if they see this kind of thing every day. I shake off my shocked expression and turn to Fantom.

"What... was... *that?*"

She shrugs, leans back in her chair, and says, "Couple of black hats. Hackers that are only interested in breakin' stuff. They get some kind of kick from ruinin' NextWorld for everyone else. Overloadin' DOTcom stores so they have to shut down. Redirectin' DOTkid doors to DOTxxx. Stupid stuff."

"I'm not talking about those hackers!" I yell a little too loudly. "I'm talking about the sword, and the killing, and the—"

"This ain't a game," Fantom says with a chuckle. "I didn't kill nobody."

"What did you do then?" Raev asks. "I've seen PvP in NextWorld, but it's inconsequential. Nothing happens. They respawn wherever they set their spawn point. But that looked... different."

Fantom leans in close and whispers, "I told you. Everything is data, yo. The sword? It's a program I wrote that forces a log-out and floods their E-Womb with spam so they can't log back in. At least not for a day or two. Simple denial of service attack. Everyone in this bar is carryin' at least one."

I look around at the other patrons feeling like I stepped into *DangerWar* without a gun.

"That avatar screamed when it happened," Xen says with a worried tone.

Fantom smirks. "I *might* have written an option or two for pain stimulus, but trust me, they deserved what they got, yo."

Xen pops two Dizzy Fizz into his mouth. Raev whispers something to him, consoling him. His hands shake.

"What's the matter?" I ask, genuinely concerned by the very real look of fear in Xen's eyes.

Raev answers for him. "He still has a hard time with... violence."

I speak before I think. "This is just NextWorld, not—"

"It doesn't matter," Raev says. "It wasn't supposed to be real in your game either, but it was. He was in a very real coma." She rubs the back of his neck with her hand. "At first meditation and the Omniversalist lessons were enough, but when you fell into a coma too..."

Xen slides another Dizzy Fizz into his mouth. His eyes roll back in his head.

I've heard of post-virtual trauma disorder before, but I always figured the people who suffered from that already had something wrong with them. Maybe they couldn't distinguish reality from virtual reality. Or maybe it was too much like something that happened in the real world.

When Xen shakes in his chair, I'm scared for him. Is this what empathy feels like? Weird.

"Sorry," Fantom says, like the word doesn't hold any weight.

"It's okay," Xen says, his voice shaking as much as his body. "It's no big deal. I'll get over it."

"You don't need to do that," Raev says, her back stiffening with an imbued strength. "You don't need to act like this is something you should be ashamed of or that you have to hide. It wasn't just a game. Something very real happened to you. It affected your body."

"It affected his mind," I say.

I can tell Raev is ready to argue, to defend her partner. I throw up both my hands to let her know I'm not looking for a fight.

"I mean, you're not wrong. It affected his body too. But it's his mind that's hurt. And that's no different in here... or out there. One affects the other."

Raev stares at me for a few seconds before I can visibly see her accept my words. Her body softens. She closes her eyes.

"You're right, Arkade. Metaversalism teaches us that who we are is not our physical form, but our hearts and our minds. Our soul has no location, it simply is." She looks at Xen with a delicate smile and says, "Your friend is pretty wise for a non-believer."

Xen smiles at me. "He believes more than he knows."

I ignore the meaningless philosophical babble and turn to Fantom. She's swiping through screens in front of her, searching for something with driven intent.

"What is it? What's happening?"

She squints her eyes, reading something on her screen as she says, "He's here."

We all sit up a little straighter and scan the room, but nothing has changed. The skeleton in the corner is still taking bets for the racing game. A tall, powerful, Amazon-looking woman is still ignoring the advances of an elf in a leather jacket. The cyborgs are still discussing something with the robots near the jukebox. An obscenely large man still sits at the bar, his avatar almost completely enveloping the bar stool underneath him, and a circle of scantily clad women are still whispering in his ear. The door hasn't opened. Nobody has entered or exited.

"I don't see him," I say as I continue to search.

I'm not looking at Fantom, but I'm sure she rolls her eyes before she says, "That's because you're lookin' for him when you should be listenin'."

"Listening? To what?"

She closes all the screens in front of her with one huge swipe and points in the air. "The song."

I listen for a few seconds to the instrumental dance beat before I ask, "What about it?"

"It's his song," she says. "He rides audio-casts."

"He travels through sound?" Xen asks, both confused and impressed.

"I told you, it's all the same. Graphics, audio, touch, taste, smell, whatever. Once you break it down, you can use it however you want."

I blink my eyes a few times to adjust to what I'm seeing. An avatar turns toward us as if he's a two-dimensional paper cut-out that I couldn't see from the side, but as he finishes the turn, he appears to be completely three-dimensional. His faceless avatar is wearing a black-and-white tuxedo with a red bow tie. His long white hair hangs far below his waist, each strand moving like a prehensile tendril.

"Fantom." He says her name with a smooth, silky tone to his voice. "Are these your friends?"

I'm surprised he doesn't look at our social screens, but I guess in a place like this, you learn not to believe what you read.

"Xen, Raev, Arkade," she says before uncomfortably clearing her throat and motioning toward the faceless avatar. "This is Worlok."

01001101

Worlok opens up his hand and a chair slides across the floor toward his waiting grip. He spins it around and sits down next to me, uncomfortably close. I push my chair away from him and a smiling mouth appears for only a second on the blank face of his avatar

"You're *the* Arkade?"

I shrug and say, "Uh. I guess?"

"Congratulations. You shot up to the top of the DOTgov Most Wanted List this morning."

"No worries, yo," Fantom says. "I logged him in on a clean account."

His smile flashes again, this time at Fantom. "I have to say, I didn't have much faith you'd be able to contact him under government lockdown. Someday you'll have to show me how you pulled that off."

I can't help wondering what someone like him would do with the power Fantom wielded over my nanomachines during my breakout.

"We need your help." Fantom says, redirecting the conversation away from her hacking skills. She bites her lip and closes her eyes like it's painful for her to say, "*I* need your help."

He leans back in his chair. "*You*? Need *my* help? I don't think I've ever heard you say those words before, much less twice in one week. Let me take a second here to appreciate this moment. I think I might—"

"We need to get into the Trash Bin."

Even without eyes, I feel his avatar's stare burning into Fantom as an uncomfortable silence hovers around the table. Xen, Raev, and I look back and forth, waiting to see which one of them will break first. When neither says anything for far too long, I break the silence.

"We're trying to find a game world that DOTgov deleted. We have the location code, but—"

He slaps his hand over my mouth, looks over his shoulder to see who's close enough to hear him and whispers, "Not here."

Without so much as a twitch of his wrist or a screen asking for our permission, the club drops away from us. We're instantly teleported into a mansion without dimensional rules. Stairways line the walls, changing direction if I look at them differently. Windows look through other windows in the same room from a different perspective. Up can be down and down can be left if I tilt my head a bit. My brain tries to wrap itself around the programming logic needed to code something like this, but my stomach twists itself into knots, throwing off my equilibrium. Twenty or so avatars sit around the room, their chairs resting on walls and ceilings. They're all manipulating screens in front of them, lost in the depths of thick code.

"Wow," Raev says, "how insane was the person that designed this place?"

Xen's mixed up eyes accept his surroundings better than any of us. "It would make for a great sermon location. We could put a DJ booth over there..."

Fantom glances around the room. "It's been a while since I've been inside Sektor's coding room."

"You blocked my invitations."

"Yeah," she says firmly. "I did."

He doesn't sound happy. "But you didn't have any problem asking me for help when you needed to—"

"I was desperate," Fantom says, cutting him off.

"Good thing I'm so nice."

"Sure," she says, cracking her knuckles, "if you want to go with that, I'll play along."

"But now you show up expecting yet another favor from me? Just like that? I'm nice, Fantom. But I'm not that nice."

Fantom rolls her eyes. Apparently there *is* someone who can annoy her as much I do.

"You've been inside the Trash Bin before."

"That was a long time ago. And it was an accident."

"You accidentally hacked into a secret domain?" Raev asks, her excitement overwhelming her ability to realize her place in the conversation.

"I was looking for a backdoor into a DOTbiz site and I stumbled across a weird connection," Worlok explains to Raev. "But they detected the intrusion right away and locked it down." He turns to me and says, "It took some serious skills for me to get away clean."

Fantom raises an eyebrow skeptically. "You're tellin' me you found a way in, a long time ago, all by yourself, but now you can't do it with an entire team of hackers helpin' you?"

He stares at her as if he's deciding whether to tell the truth.

She steps closer to him and places her hand on his chest. "This is important, yo."

It looks like he's getting lost in her sad eyes for a second, but he pulls himself away. "I'm not going to waste my time on a hack like that just to steal some game."

She steps toward him, shaking her head. "We're not stealin' some deleted game. We're tryin' to save somethin' that's... that's..."

"What?" he asks softly when he realizes she's not just being dramatic to fake the importance. "What are you trying to save?"

"It's not *what* we're trying to save," I say. "It's *who*."

His head tilts with even more confusion.

Fantom grabs his chin and turns it back toward her. "The game that trapped me. *DangerWar 2*. I know you've read about it."

He looks at me and then flashes Fantom a devious smile, like he knows a dirty little secret that amuses him.

"Yeah. I *may* have heard of it."

"Then you know the rumors. The artificial intelligence..."

"Yeah. They said it was so advanced it actually fooled some players. Big deal."

"It's not like that, yo. It wasn't foolin' them. It was learnin' from them."

I can hear the recognition as he repeats, "Learning?" He glances at us again, searching each of us, trying to find one of us that doesn't believe what she's saying. There's a calm honesty on all our faces. We patiently wait for him to catch up to the truth.

"You're telling me that you think an NPC in that game acquired artificial consciousness?"

"Not one. Thousands, yo."

Another fact slaps him in the face. He mentally stumbles for a second as Fantom keeps talking, trying to keep him on the track that she wants him to be on.

"Think about that, Worlok. Think about what something like that could mean for the powers-that-be. Think about what it could mean to the public that believes DOTgov can control NextWorld. This is the ultimate show of information freedom. They're tryin' to delete the most important data ever created, because *they* can't control it."

He continues to deny her line of thinking. "Even if I could get you in... you have no idea how big that place is, how much stuff users delete every day. You'd never find a single, specific game in time."

"We have fourteen hours," she says, gesturing toward him to share the same timer that's sitting in the corner of all our views.

He replies condescendingly, "You don't get it. You'd never be able to find—"

"And we have the location code."

"How did you—"

"I got a guy," she says with a smile.

Worlok stiffens. "A *guy*?"

Fantom rolls her eyes. "It ain't like that. He's just a guy. But he's legit, yo."

"Yeah. I'm sure he is."

Something changes in Worlok. I don't understand it. It's so sudden. He steps away from Fantom, crossing his arms and acting smug again.

"Please, Worlok."

"Fine, Fantom. I'll get you a hack, *again.* A nice little doorway into the Trash Bin."

She doesn't seem convinced, but she says, "Thank you. I appreciate your—"

"But this time it's going to cost you." I hear him smack his lips together, even though his face has no mouth. "Let's say... 250,000 credits. And that's the friend discount."

She jerks her head back with a look of surprised confusion, like he's speaking in a different language.

"Credits? You want *credits*?"

"Yeah, Fantom. I want credits. You think I'm going to hand over another hack because you show up and bat your eyelashes? Think again, girl. Your avatar ain't *that* cute."

The muscles in her arms flex as she squeezes both hands into fists. "You pompous little..." She takes a deep breath. "This has never been about credits for you, yo. This is about the revolution. This is about stickin' it to DOTgov and exposin' the truth."

Worlok lifts his hands and shrugs. "Yeah, well, what can I say? Revolutions are expensive."

"You know I ain't never been a thief, yo. If you think I'm goin' to be stealin' from bank accounts for you—"

"No," he says firmly. "I need clean credits."

"Clean? Where are you expectin' me to come up with 250,000 credits?"

He turns away. "I don't care. Maybe you can ask your *guy*."

The inside of Sektor's warped code room drops away and we're slammed back into Club L33T. We're all sitting around the same table. Except for Worlok.

"He seems real great," I say to Fantom. "I can see why you partnered up with him. You two are a lot alike."

"Shut up."

"He still has feelings for you," Xen says. "Maybe if you just—"

"I said *shut up*."

Raev leans forward and whispers, "Where are we going to come up with that many credits?"

"What about your mother?" Fantom asks. "Would she lend you credits if you asked real nice-like?"

"Sure," Raev says. "All I have to do is renounce my religion, end my partnership, and get a job at InfoLock. Then maybe..."

"What about you?" I ask Xen. "Your church looked like it was bringing in a pretty steady tithe from your congregation."

"Sorry, Kade," he says weakly. "You know if I could, I'd give you every last credit I have, but it doesn't work that way. I don't have direct access to the account. Every credit I spend requires verification by the church to ensure there's no corruption. What comes in to the church, I have to spend on the church. Nothing else. *I'm* not rich. The church is."

I look at the timer. Less than fourteen hours left. As every second drops out, the impending doom in my chest grows. Cyren is getting further and further away.

"Once he hacks this doorway for us," Raev asks, "can't we steal it from him?"

"Raev!" Xen whisper-shouts, appalled that she could consider something like that.

"What?" she says, throwing up her hands. "We're sitting in a club for hackers, talking about how we're going to pay a cyberterrorist to help us steal a game world from a secret DOTgov domain. It's not like anything we're doing here is exactly legal."

"We can't steal from Worlok," Fantom says. "It's killin' me to admit it, but he's the best hacker I know. He might be the best hacker, period. I ain't got no hope of crackin' his encryptions. Even if I could, eventually he'd find us. And Worlok ain't exactly the forgivin' type."

We all sit in silence, wracking our brains, trying to come up with a solution. Music pumps in the back ground. Murmurs and whispers of criminal activities swarm around the club. Seconds tick away.

"I'll get the credits," I say, pushing myself away from the table and standing up.

"How?" Raev asks. "Where?"

I flip up the collar on my leather trench coat and say, "Koins."

"Koins?"

"They sell for credits in the DOTcom auctions."

"That account ain't got any Koins," Fantom says, dismissing me with a wave of her hand. "And we don't have time for me to try cleaning your old account enough for you to access your inventory."

"I can get Koins."

"How are you gonna do that, yo?"

"He's going to play games," Xen says to them without taking his eyes off of me. "Right? You're going to log-in to DOTfun, and you're going to play games."

"Yeah, Xen. I'm going to play games," I say as I straighten my cowboy hat, peering out from under the brim. "And then I'm going to save Cyren."

01001110

We skim across the edge of DOTorg on Fantom's flying carpet. The domain is full of protesters of every sort. Some are asking for better wages, some are asking for better tasting vitapaste, some are asking for time restrictions on DOTfun. They remain in their designated sites inside the domain, yelling as loudly as they can, yet they are heard by no one.

As we fly over a group of mothers with picket signs trying to raise the age restrictions of mind-altering downloads, Fantom asks, "How are you plannin' on makin' 250,000 credits? We ain't got the time to—"

"I'm going to shoot people."

"I think you might need a more sophisticated plan than that," Raev says through a chuckle.

"I'm going to shoot a *lot* of people."

"I'll be helpin' you make those credits," Fantom says as we cross over the information superhighway. "And I don't want none of this 'I can do it on my own' nonsense."

"I appreciate that."

Everyone pauses for a second, confused by my unusually good nature, but I'm already planning battle strategies.

"We're helping too," Xen says.

"I thought you weren't dealing well with violence? I don't want you to freak out in the middle of a gunfight."

Xen glances at the floor, nervously sliding another Dizzy Fizz into his mouth. "I don't have to play the same games as you to win Koins. I've been getting good at flying planes in this simulator. It's actually kind of neat. You have to—"

"You sure you can fly with all those Dizzy Fizz apps in your system?"

He lets out a laugh. "I might need a few more before I'm stupid enough to climb in to a cockpit."

I focus on the horizon instead of his words, waiting for the DOTfun domain to appear. "Do whatever you need to do. I'm playing solo."

Xen exchanges a hurt look with Raev, who offers him a look of understanding or sympathy or something. I don't know.

"I mean, you have to understand where I'm coming from," I say without knowing what's upsetting them. "We have a limited amount of time. I'm good at solo play. I know that. But the group stuff? It takes time. It takes practice. We don't have that luxury."

They keep looking out of the corner of their eyes at each other like they're afraid to tell me what they're all thinking.

I change the subject. "Has Raev played games in DOTfun before?"

"Sure," she says. "Mostly role-playing games. I was always the healer in the group, which means I was totally underappreciated, but whatever."

She's saying something, trying to make some kind of point, but I don't have the time to decipher it.

"Don't worry," Raev continues, "I can farm materials that people use for their crafting skills in those games and sell them for Koins."

"Even if we're not playing the same games," Xen says, "we're still a group."

"Truth" is all Fantom says as she holds up one hand balled in a fist.

I look at all of them. My friends. The people who mean more to me than my own family. Internally, I acknowledge everything they're doing for me. Every choice they're making. Every risk they're taking. Every sacrifice they're... sacrificing. But I can't think of a way to sum it all up. What do people say in situations like this? What's the proper way to say thank you? Do I give a big, heart-wrenching, awe-inspiring speech about how much they mean to me? Do I individually acknowledge how much each step they took with me helped me reach my goal? I don't know.

All I can come up with is "Cool."

Everyone acts like they're satisfied with my response, so I choose to move forward, unable to justify the time needed to analyze the social interaction.

When the flying carpet crests the horizon of DOTorg, I can see the first graphical representations of DOTfun. Not much has changed besides a few minor improvements to the polygon levels and some random new NPCs. There's a nostalgic excitement that beats in my chest when the constant display of fireworks explodes over the entrance and the wacky assortment of NPCs greet us as we settle into the queue waiting to enter. There's something about the arrangement of everything. Even the smell of stale blood and fresh gunpowder that surround the combat games creates this potpourri that brings me back to a hundred afternoons spent here after DOTedu.

Xen turns to me as we enter the domain and asks, "What game are you—"

"*DangerWar*," I answer before he finishes the question.

"You sure, yo?" Fantom asks.

I nod silently.

"There's been a lot of new games released in the last couple years. We could be playin' somethin' more popular."

"I don't have time to learn a new rule set or gun type accuracy or any of the other factors that could alter my play style. I need to stick with what I know in order to maximize my Koin collecting."

Fantom banks the carpet to the left and we fly over one of the more popular race tracks, the same one being bet on in Club L33T. We drop Xen and Raev off at their respective game worlds, then dive toward the gates to *DangerWar*. They look bigger than before, but I'm sure they haven't changed. There's still the giant title bolted on to the forty-foot-high arches, and there's still the blank wall that's missing the wooden door leading to *DangerWar 2*, and there's still the group of players mingling with each other outside, just not as many. They're all waiting to meet other players or bragging about their latest kill or just rethinking their strategies before they head back in to the game.

A few people take notice of us landing, and a few of them take a second glance when they see my avatar. Arkade was far from the only cowboy in NextWorld, so as soon as they look at the social screen connected to the ghost account, they go back to ignoring me.

"Got any tips, yo?" Fantom asks as we make our way through the crowd. "I never played the first one."

I shrug my shoulders and say, "Kill them before they kill you."

Fantom rolls her eyes. "Do you want to succeed or not?"

"Of course I do. I'm just—"

"You're actin' arrogant, that's what you're doin'. It's time to grow up, Cowboy. How about you offer me a real answer?"

I open my mouth to argue, then suck in a breath and say, "Okay. You're right. I'm sorry." I stop and think. "We don't have time to go over the map layouts... that's probably the biggest advantage I have. I know where the weapon drops are. I know where the secret passages are. I know where the traps are. I've played this game a thousand times."

"Wow," Fantom says. "I'm so impressed, yo."

"No," I say, shaking my head. "I'm not... I mean, I'm trying to say that you're going to have to find weapons on the people you kill. This isn't like the sequel. You start with a pistol and you have to find better stuff, or buy better stuff with Koins... which we aren't going to do because we're going to save every Koin we get."

"You can get different weapons? Why did they change that in the sequel? That's way more fun, yo."

I shrug and say, "Sometimes sequels aren't as good as the original."

"So how do we get Koins?"

"By killing them before they kill you."

Fantom lets out a long, annoyed sigh.

"I'm serious! Your kill to death ratio, how many kills you score compared to how many times you die, determines the payout at the end of the match."

Fantom glances down at the timer in front of her and says, "We have just over thirteen hours. Takin' into account havin' to contact Worlok, not to mention goin' to the Trash Bin and cuttin' the NPCs out of the game world... I'm thinkin' we got a maximum of ten hours, yo."

"Fine. Ten hours." I turn toward the familiar gate and speak through clenched teeth. "Now let's go shoot something."

01001111

As soon as the game appears around me, I smile. I recognize the map right away. The Haunted Mansion. It's the last map that I played in, so it's a fitting way to return.

I spawn in the graveyard, standing next to a sarcophagus. I inhale the familiar scent of dead leaves and look up at the moon peeking out from behind some wispy clouds. I was expecting the overwhelming nostalgia of the game, but what I wasn't expecting is how bad everything looks. The graphics appear jagged and plain compared to *DangerWar 2*, which is weird because I used to think they looked amazing. Everything looks like a game, like a graphical representation of reality. Even the cold chill in the air doesn't feel like real cold air. But that's okay. It helps me stay focused. It helps me treat this like the task that it is, not some fun escape or outlet for my hostility.

I need Koins. That's it.

I spin around to the front of the sarcophagus and shoot at the chain that's locked across the door. A few bullets chip away at it until it breaks free. I give the stone door a shove and step inside. Caskets line the wall. I know that inside each one is a zombie NPC waiting to grab me, but the third one from the left is different. I slide the top of the casket to the side and find a large machete laying

159

inside. As soon as I pick it up, a sheath appears on my belt and I slide the blade into it.

When I step back out from the sarcophagus, bullets whiz past my head. One strikes me in the arm before I'm able to jump behind a large tombstone. At first I think the gunfire is semi-automatic, but from the sound of the shots, I realize that it's a bolt-action rifle, which makes me nervous. The player has to be experienced if they're firing so quickly.

I check my arm. It's bleeding, but it won't kill me. I poke my head out from behind the tombstone and peer through the thick fog, searching for the muzzle flare when the player fires again. It flashes from the other side of the graveyard, near the cellar door at the base of the mansion. I duck back behind the tombstone, watching stone fragments fly into the air as the attacker continues to fire.

I smile and wait.

Soon enough, the gunfire stops. They ran out of ammunition. I know the person firing at me is dropping the magazine from the rifle and pulling another one from their inventory, and that's just the opportunity I was waiting for.

I spin out from behind the tombstone and run across the graveyard, directly at the other player. I pound my feet into the soft soil underneath me, trying to close the gap between us. My pistol is good from about twenty yards. Any farther than that and the accuracy degrades as well as the damage.

The attacker is covered in leaves and twigs, with pointed ears like a wood nymph. I think she meant the scantily clad look of her avatar to distract the male players of the game. Of course there's also the chance that she *is* a male player in real life.

She's struggling to get the fresh magazine into the rifle, panicking when she sees me charging her. I wait until I can see the whites of her eyes before I pull the trigger. Her head rocks back. I catch the rifle flying from her hands as her body slumps against the ground and dissipates into a puddle of pixels. The name "Bunnee" appears in front of me and a red mark slashes across it.

Without ammunition, the rifle is worthless to me in combat, so I slip it into my inventory. I'll trade it for Koins later.

I don't waste time. I throw open the cellar doors, slash through the thick cobwebs with my machete, and descend into the underground portion of the map. Torches flicker against the stone walls. I hear the clang of metal in the distance, then a large boom shakes the ceiling. Dust and rock fall around me.

When I turn a corner, there's a groundskeeper walking toward me with a shovel. He's an NPC. I know that if I kill him, he's got a key in his pocket that gives me access to a secret passageway through the hedge maze outside. I raise my gun. He stares at me, blankly, waiting for the kill. My trigger finger starts to squeeze, but I can't do it.

He's not Cyren. I know that. He'll never be anything like her. His code is primitive compared to the NPCs in *DangerWar 2*. He'll never think for himself. He'll never learn anything other than what his programming tells him. He'll never be self-aware. As soon as the deathmatch is over, he'll disappear. But I still can't kill him. He's too close, too much like the NPCs I've sworn to protect. I run past him and turn toward the wine cellar, leaving the thoughtless avatar behind me.

I flinch when a caveman comes running down the hall. He lifts a laser gun at me and fires, but I'm already leaping on to the floor. The lasers fly over the top of me as I land on my belly and fire at him. The bullet strikes his kneecap and he tumbles on to the floor before he gets another shot off. As soon as he lifts his head, I fire again, this time striking him right between the eyes. He explodes into pixels. I lift myself off the floor and run for the laser gun. As soon as I pick it up, another avatar comes around the corner and I realize what the caveman was running from.

I hear a chainsaw sputtering before I see Fantom step into the torchlight. She smiles when she sees me and launches at me, screaming like a maniac and lifting the weapon above her head. I suppose it's meant to intimidate me, or make me hesitate so she can close the gap between us, but I lift the laser gun and fire. The red beam burns right through her chest and pixels spill across the floor.

For a second, I'm pleased with myself. I always wondered if I could win in a fight against Fantom, but then I realize that she may have handed me her death for the Koins, choosing the loud melee weapon just to go out in a blaze of glory.

I put the chainsaw in my inventory and look down at the side of the laser gun. There's a nice amount of battery power left in the high-damage weapon, so I put my starter pistol in my inventory and continue through the lower levels of the mansion.

I find an avatar with a jack o' lantern head. He's dual-wielding pistols, but he's got his back to me so he doesn't even know who kills him. I find a grizzly bear beating a knight with nunchaku on the stairs leading to the ground floor. My laser burns through both of them in one shot. In the dining room there's a pirate with a shark's head that gives me a bit of trouble because he's launching buzzsaws out of a mechanical cannon. I manage to burn off his arm with a lucky shot and he's forced to drop his weapon. After that it's an easy kill.

I'm hyper-focused. Cyren's escape drives me, fueling my violent rampage through the map. One by one they fall, and soon enough the game is announcing the name of my ghost account as the winner. I know I won't be earning any glory as long as I'm using this account, but I'm not here to coddle my pride. I'm here for the kills. I'm here for the Koins. I'm here for Cyren.

The master bedroom where I killed the final player falls away and I'm left floating in the mists of the game menu. Screens appear all around me with the statistics from the game. Koins pour out of the sky, falling into the treasure chest inside my inventory, but I don't wait to count them. I select the next map.

I'm ignoring the growling in my stomach and the insistence of my bladder. They're telling me to log-out and take care of my real world needs, but there's no time for that. I need to take advantage of every second I have and grab as many Koins as I can.

I need to shoot. I need to kill. I need to win.

01010000

Each map bleeds into the next. I'm killing players on the surface of the moon. I'm killing players in the muddy trenches of an ancient battlefield. I'm killing players in a shopping mall. I'm killing players in desert wasteland. Each death makes way for the next. Familiar faces appear over and over as the same players continue their attempts to beat me. But they never do.

At first I think I'm getting lucky, but then I realize the difference between them and me. They're still having fun. They're still playing a game. This isn't fun for me anymore. I'm not taking my time. I'm not admiring the graphics. I'm working a game world to meet an end. I'm making constant calculations of distance and movement and speed in order to win as fast as I can, kill as many players as I can, and collect as many Koins as I can. Which player do I kill first? Do I pick off the weak ones and let the better players clear the map for me, or do I try to increase my kill-to-death ratio by taking out the strong players first, leaving the weak ones for me to rack up kills with? Do I use that box of grenades I found or do I trade it for credits? Do I use stealth tactics or shock-and-awe bravado? There are a million questions that I must answer instantaneously, without second-guessing myself.

No matter how drawn into the game I am, I'm always hyper-aware of Cyren's absence. I'm incomplete without her. I'm lopsided, drifting away from my own center. I need her to tell me it's going to be okay. I need her to calm my mind, my racing thoughts. I need her smile, her embrace, those simple words of hers that always make everything so clear, so vivid. I miss her fighting by my side, but those thoughts bring me right back into the action, because I know I'm doing it all for her.

I can't save the same Cyren that I knew, that exact consciousness, but I can still save the possibility of her, the potential of her. Maybe she'll grow into someone greater. That thought gives me comfort.

The timer counts down faster and faster as my treasure chest fills with Koins. I never waste the briefest of moments to check the number. It doesn't matter. I keep doing the best that I can, and when it's all over, I have to hope it's enough.

When the timer reaches the mark telling me that I've been playing for ten straight hours, I finish the map I'm on. I hack off the Rhinoceros head of an avatar with a battleaxe on the bridge of a starship and the game ends. The map falls away and I log-out from the menu. I appear outside the *DangerWar* gates and see the group waiting for me.

Xen rushes over with a large smile, his body wobbling with every hurried step. He swipes his menu toward me, sharing the Koins that the rest of the group made.

"Did we do it? Did we make enough? What am I saying? Of course we did. Right?"

"Give him a chance to breathe," Raev says as she catches up to Xen. Then she turns to me and asks, "But seriously... did we make enough?"

"I don't know," I say after I check my inventory and see the grand total. "And I won't know until we put it in an auction and see what people are willing to pay."

"We don't have time for chattin', yo," Fantom says as she summons her flying carpet. "Let's go."

Raev helps Xen on to the back of the rug. With his wobbly stance, he's barely able to stand up straight. We take off into the skies over DOTfun and bank toward the super-highway that leads toward DOTcom.

I must not be hiding my anxiety well, because it doesn't take long for Fantom to lean over and say, "I'm sure it will be enough. There's always people willin' to part with credits to get a head start in new games."

"I know. I just hope they sell quickly."

Fantom slaps the carpet and says, "If it weren't for Worlok bein' so greedy, we wouldn't be in this mess. He was never like this before. Credits were the last thing he was thinkin' about. He used to be..."

I'm not sure if she doesn't finish her sentence because she can't think of the right word to describe what he used to be, or if she gets lost in the memory of what he used to be. Her eyes drift off toward the horizon.

I try to picture Fantom in a partnership, but I can't. It's hard to picture the cold, headstrong woman cuddling up next to someone. I have to imagine she often butted heads with the egotistical hacker she called a partner. Perhaps they were too similar, unable to balance each other out. Too much fire and not enough water. Both of them ones and neither of them zeros.

As we cross over the last of the thousand-lanes connecting NextWorld, I can see DOTcom in the distance. The carpet speeds up to its maximum bandwidth and we dive toward the city of flashing advertisements.

Where the companies of DOTbiz might save credits on design and detail, looking exactly the same no matter what street you drive down, DOTcom is where they spend those credits showing off. The domain is a mess of animations and avatars, screens and pop-up video-casts. There is no logical rhyme or reason to the shapes or buildings other than to draw attention.

Our carpet slows to a crawl as Fantom's ad-blockers run in overtime, trying to keep our view as clear as possible. I lose track of our location, lost in the maze of offers, coupons, and sales. This is an intentional effect, designed to keep you occupied in the domain for as long as you have credits to spend. Luckily, Fantom's directional software leads us through the most expensive, outer banners, and directly into the auction houses.

"We need to choose wisely," I say, glancing around at hundreds of different spheres, boxes, towers, and landscapes, all offering their services to anyone looking to get rid of some inventory.

"Yeah," Fantom says. "They're all goin' to take their cut. It's gonna take time to compare them all and figure out which one takes the least while still having enough members to give us a good price."

Xen pokes his head between us and flashes a goofy smile. "I believe I can help with that."

"How?" I ask with an annoyed skepticism.

He points at the largest auction house, TraderZone, a glowing obelisk that towers over the entire area. The hottest items cover the outer walls of the structure and most of the traffic in the domain focuses on that particular entrance. It's the most well-known and the most well-used site. It's the easiest, most user-friendly auction house, offering to take care of every function of the transaction. It's where every mom and dad and grandparent who doesn't know the ins and outs of NextWorld go to sell their junk. It's where every business trades out their overstocked virtual warehouses. It's also the most expensive auction house, taking forty percent of any profit in exchange for the ease of use.

"Are you crazy? We're *not* using TraderZone. After they take their cut, I'd be lucky to clear 150,000 credits," I say, looking away from him as if his suggestion isn't worth any more discussion.

Xen sets his hand on my shoulder to gain my attention again and looks at me through his drooping eyes. "Kade, at some point you're going to have to trust me."

I glance at Fantom, but she offers me a shrug, waiting for my reply. I look back into Xen's eyes, his smile glowing with a warmth that's both innocent and powerful. His inebriated mind doesn't make me feel safe. I don't trust this new Xen. I don't trust the fog that hangs over his mind. But I look at Raev and she offers me a confident nod. I'm surprised when I realize that it's her I trust.

When this is all over, I'll have the time to help Xen. I'll help him come back from wherever he is. But for now, she's the one keeping him in line, keeping him upright, until we can find a way to help him. Until we can find a way to heal his mind.

I take a deep breath and nod at Fantom. She sighs with reluctance and turns the carpet toward the entrance at the bottom of the giant obelisk, allowing the flow of traffic to swallow our carpet.

As we pass through the doorway into the brightly-lit interior, Fantom squints her eyes and says, "Let's make some credits, yo."

01010001

The auction house is disgustingly huge. Even with the immense amount of traffic flowing in and out of the site, there's no need for the size other than to appear grandiose. I grimace at the garishness of every sign, confused by the font choices and color schemes, as well as the glaringly obvious operational flaws. It's as if they fired someone who used a minimalist approach and hired a different designer to splash his showy, ostentatious choices right on top. I rub my eyes and decide that instead of nit-picking every error and determining how I'd fix it, I'll place my judgments aside and focus on the task at hand.

I notice Fantom giving me a nervous look as we creep through the main floor. We're berated by NPC auctioneers trying to sell the wares of their customers by yelling at us from floating booths that circle the site.

I turn around and glare at a smiling Xen. "So? Now what?"

Xen opens up a screen in front of him and selects a choice without saying a word. I glance at Raev, who appears to be as calm and collected as Xen, peering around the site as if she were sight-seeing or window-shopping. Their tranquility grates on my own anxiety, causing it to boil over.

"What's the plan, Xen?" I yell over the loud announcements of an NPC right next to our floating carpet who's offering me a great deal on a virtual apartment.

Xen holds up a finger and winks at me. It drives me crazy. We're running out of time. He should be freaking out. *Everyone* should be freaking out.

My head jerks forward when we come to a sudden stop. A floating platform descends from above, slowing in front of the carpet. Standing atop the platform is an NPC auctioneer with a three-piece suit and a mustache that curls up on either side.

"Hello and welcome to TraderZone, where *your* trash is *someone's* treasure! How may I assist you today?"

I'm about to open my mouth when Xen leans past me and flashes a card that he pulls from his inventory. The NPC leans forward and studies the text.

"I see that you qualify for our non-profit-religion exemption program. I'm pleased to accept your use of our services today, free of charge."

Fantom and I glance at each other, then turn and look at Xen with disbelief.

He holds up his hands and smiles. "What?"

"I thought you said there were strict rules to stop any kind of corruption in the church."

He pops a pill between his lips, his eyelids hang low over his eyes, and he mumbles, "We're not in church."

I glance at Raev who takes a deep breath in through her nose and says, "Metaversalism teaches us that to deny a gift is to deny love."

I raise an eyebrow. "I don't know if I'd call subverting a loophole in a government program a 'gift.'"

Fantom smirks and says, "Maybe they've been hangin' out with me a little too much, yo."

Xen scratches his chin and without losing his smile he says, "I'll have to meditate upon this course of action and determine whether this was an accurate translation of the lesson..."

"Later, my love," Raev says as she pats him on the back. "There's always time for that later."

"Yes, of course," he says with a wink. "Later."

I turn back to the NPC and offer our Koins to him. He places them in a temporary storage and yells out like a battle cry, "Profit!" as his floating platform spins into the air.

"And now we wait," Fantom says.

She pulls the carpet to the right and parks it near a concession stand selling digital food and drinks. My stomach growls in the real world when I smell the fried foods. I instinctively rub my belly and Fantom notices.

"You should log-out. Eat."

I shake my head and look away. "I can eat after we finish this."

Raev places her hand on my back and says, "A bit of vitapaste may give you the strength you need."

"It does a body good," Xen says as he tosses three pills into his mouth at once.

"I'll be fine."

I don't want to admit the truth. I don't want to admit how scared I am of the real world. I don't want to admit how frightened I am of leaving my virtual existence again. I don't want to feel the cold of the tower room. I don't want to face the harsh glare of the artificial sunlight. I don't want to see my real face looking back at me in the reflective screen above the sink. But most of all, I'm afraid that if I leave, I won't be able to come back.

It's not logical. Fantom has assured me that she has everything under control. She assured me that Ekko's tower room is perfectly safe. Her algorithms and protocol bypasses divert my signal in so many directions that tracing my actions would be like finding a needle in a haystack of needles. None of this means that my fear disappears.

I watch Xen slide some more pills between his lips. His eyelids become heavier and heavier, slowly shutting as his head rests against Raev's shoulder.

"Do you think it's a good idea for him to be downloading so many of those apps?"

The question startles her. She glances down at Xen's face and smiles.

"Just look at him."

"I am. He looks... sick."

She runs her hand lightly across his cheek.

"No," she says. "He looks calm. You didn't see what he was like... before. It's like you said, his mind was broken when he died in that game. He suffered from nightmares and panic attacks every day. If the pills help him..."

"Downloading inebriation software isn't going to cure him of anything. It's just making him weaker."

She looks uncomfortable, like I'm challenging something she's not ready to face.

"You think I don't want him to get better? You think I don't want him to think clearly again? You think I don't want to look into his eyes and see the man I fell in love with?"

At first, I can't help connect the dots to Cyren. This new Cyren that I'm trying to save. It feels like what Raev is describing is so similar to what I'm afraid of happening to Cyren. Is the virus that stole her from me any different than the apps that Xen is downloading? They've both changed the people we love into unrecognizable faces.

But Cyren didn't choose that virus. Every time Xen puts one of those things in his mouth, there's a moment he can still be saved.

"I don't know what to do," she continues. "The church needs him too. We've been relying on prerecorded sermons for longer than I care to admit. Our congregation is shrinking every day because there's nothing new. They want *him* to lead, *his* words, *his* music." She shakes her head, rethinking her sentence. "But Metaversalism teaches us to support our partner, even when they fall."

"You aren't supporting him. You're letting him lie on the ground."

"I'm respecting his choice," she says and I can see the anger in her eyes. "Reality is too much for him right now. It's too hard. He made a choice to escape." Her eyes flash at me like darts. "Didn't *he* support *you* when you made the same choice?"

"I wasn't—"

Before I can reply, a bell rings above us. Xen's eyes flash open and he sits up straight, searching for the source of the noise. The auctioneer floats down and opens a screen with a number on it.

"You've received a bid for 265,000 credits!"

"Accept!" I shout.

Xen slaps his palm against the accept button on the screen.

"Congratulations on your successful auction. Would you like to participate in a quick survey to help improve our services?"

Fantom yanks on the front of the carpet and we lift off, zooming over the heads of the auctioneers and firing through the exit, into the glossy, flashy domain of DOTcom. We skim between two animated billboards featuring competing dating services and turn toward DOTnet.

I want to keep arguing with Raev, to make her understand, but I push it away. There will be time for that later. I'll help Xen and fix everything once Cyren is safe.

It only takes a few minutes for us to reach DOTnet, but I'm counting every second. My anxiety tries to push the carpet faster, closer to our goal.

She's so close.

We enter the sewers underneath the domain and our carpet slides into the tunnels. Fantom opens up a screen and sends a simple audio-cast to Worlok.

"We got your credits."

It takes a few panic-inducing seconds, but he finally responds with a teleport. The tunnel drops away and his surrealist hacker house slams into view. We're standing in a room that twists as you look further into it. Worlok is standing dead center.

"I'm impressed," he says, slapping me on the back even though he's in front of me. "You must be an awfully good gamer to get that many Koins in a few hours."

"I don't have time to talk about how impressed you are." I swipe my hand across my inventory and toss the credits into a trade screen. "Just take your credits and give us the doorway."

"Sorry, but it's not that easy. I can't just hand you a doorway and expect you to turn the knob. This is a serious hack, and unless you've got the time to spend learning my program, I'll have to lead you through."

I glance at Fantom, unsure if this is normal or not. I figure she can see through his lies better than I can. She nods at me, confirming the need for his assistance, but she doesn't look happy about it.

"Good," he says and even without an actual face, I can hear his smile in his voice. He's excited by what's about to happen. "First, you're all going to need key markers in your inventory to let the program know you have access to the entry point."

He pulls something from his inventory and opens his hand, offering us a small pile of keys. We all step forward and pick up one of the antique looking objects. They're made of a tarnished iron, with an intricate design at the top. I spin mine around upright to see it better. The iron work wraps around itself, creating a logo with two question marks back to back.

Just like the logo printed on the virus.

01010010

I lunge for Worlok. My arms thrust out like grappling hooks, reaching for his neck. He doesn't flinch. This is his world. The vertigo of the room throws me to the side. The gravity of the ceiling slams me upward.

I should have known better, but I'm not thinking straight. I don't want to think anymore. I don't want to hurt anymore. I want to act.

"What are you doin', yo?" Fantom steps between me and Worlok as I climb back to my feet.

"It was his virus that deleted the game." The words burn inside my throat. Tears, like hot acid, run from my eyes. My head is swimming. "He killed her."

I leap at him again, but this time Fantom stops me. With one hand she snatches me from the air, her fingers wrapping around my throat.

"You're actin' crazy, yo. Worlok is our only chance of savin' her."

"This is *his* fault!" I'm trying to scream through my crying, "That symbol! Those question marks. That's his logo. That's what he puts on his apps, right?"

"Hackers like to leave their mark," Fantom says, oddly quiet. "At least the arrogant ones."

"It was on the virus," I growl, my eyes burning white hot hate into Worlok. "He made it. He created the thing that took her away from me."

Fantom sets me down, but she holds up a single finger in front of my face, telling me to stop. Worlok crosses his arms and leans against a wall, as if he's bored by my accusations. Fantom glances at him, but he offers her nothing other than a shrug of his shoulders. If he had a mouth, I'd kick in every one of his teeth.

"I take it you haven't told him your role in all of this?" Worlok says, his faceless head turning toward Fantom.

She's staring at the floor with a look that I've never seen her make. It's shame.

"What's he talking about?" Xen asks.

"Yes, Fantom," Worlok says, allowing a grin to appear on his face. "What *am* I talking about?"

My mouth is hanging open, waiting for her silence to end.

"I had to save you," she mumbles.

My voice is low and steady when I ask, "What do you mean? What did you do?"

She flashes Worlok a look of anger.

I grab a hold of her arm.

"What did you do?"

"It started with the parent groups. They were protestin' your entrapment in the world. They didn't think it was right what DOTgov was doin'. They were startin' to question whether DOTfun was safe for their own children. Normally that stuff gets lost in DOTorg. No one pays attention. But the gamer news-casts were still interested in you. Still interested in your story. People started askin' questions. Too many questions."

She pulls her arm from my grip. "I read the files in DOTgov, I listened to the conversations. When you fell into the coma, they ran out of excuses. They were going to pull the plug, yo."

She points her finger in my face. "You saved my life! I couldn't just sit back and watch them kill you."

I'm unable to catch up to the truth. My lips try to form words, but I only mumble, "You killed her."

"No. I didn't. What I did was choose to save you first. She's still alive, Cowboy. I'm goin' to save both of you."

"You put that virus in our world and you—"

"Actually, the virus was *my* idea," Worlok brags. "When Fantom came to me for help, I wasn't sure it was possible to get you out. But I knew that if I completely deleted the game world, there would be nothing left to interface with your nanomachines. They'd be able to do a cold reboot of your E-Womb without anything to cause feedback. There would be nothing interacting with you to fry your brain. Course, then I had to find a way to get the virus inside the game world. Every stream between *DangerWar 2* and NextWorld was locked down... until you requested that video-cast. Like a Trojan horse, I hid the worm inside the stream and," he flashes me a smile, "ta da! Here you are."

I burst toward him, my fists flinging and lashing out in a crazy swirl of psychotic violence. I'm losing it, my emotions are exploding and I have no way to contain them. But while we're inside his private site, Worlok doesn't even need to move. I'm thrown to the floor immediately.

"You killed her," I say, weeping into the wood floor. "You destroyed the most important thing in the world to me."

He turns to Fantom, deciding I'm not worth trying to communicate with. Fantom nods to him and leans down next to me.

"DOTgov was done makin' excuses to the media. They were done tryin' to convince parents that NextWorld was safe for their kids. They were goin' to shut down the game world *and* your mind. I didn't have any other choice."

I feel betrayed. My emotions are so overwhelming that I can't look at anything logically. I'm hearing what Fantom is saying, and I'm sure a part of me knows that she isn't the enemy. What she did was the best option in a lose/lose scenario. But I'll never admit that risking Cyren's life for my own was the right choice, even though Cyren made the same choice.

"You don't have to forgive me, Cowboy. But you're goin' to need my help if you want to get her back."

"If what you've told me is true," Worlok says, "and these NPCs are actually capable of learning, then they belong in NextWorld anyway, not trapped in some game."

Raev sets her hand on my shoulder. "Think about what Cyren will be able to accomplish in NextWorld."

I don't care if it's better. I want everything to be back to the way it was. I want the Cyren I knew back. I want her to love me again.

Xen touches my other shoulder and says, "Metaversalism teaches us that we can't go back, we can't change the past. We can only change the future. We need to move forward and choose the right actions in order to secure our vision of the life we want."

I'm worried about my own ability to rationalize when Xen starts making sense. But he's right, of course. It's tempting to lose myself in memories. I want to close my eyes and dream of her again, next to me, her black lips smiling, but I don't have time for that. I don't have time to get lost in this ache that's threatening to take me over. I need to act. I need to complete my quest.

I straighten my cowboy hat, slide my fingers across the brim, and with a deep breath, I reboot my mind. I put my emotions where they can't hurt me and lock my brain back on to the task at hand. I step up closer to Worlok and Fantom. Everyone jerks, expecting me to lash out again. But I don't. If I've learned anything, it's that I need to accept the help that someone else can offer me. I can't play solo.

"I need your help." It may be the hardest thing I've ever said. Right or wrong doesn't matter to me right now. Only her. Only Cyren. "But if this doesn't work, if anything happens to her..."

Worlok silently accepts the terms of my halfhearted peace offering. He pulls his long white hair behind his faceless head and cracks every one of his knuckles.

"Let's hack."

01010011

It's the last thing I care to admit, but I can see why Fantom thinks Worlok might be the best hacker in NextWorld. Deep in the cavernous tunnels below DOTnet, he maneuvers through menus with both hands like he's conducting an orchestra. Dual-wielding programs, he assesses and exploits vulnerabilities in the security with simple gestures, flicking wrists and twisting fingers in a digital dance. There's a driven passion to his movements, but I can tell that he loves every second of it.

Fantom assists him, throwing out her own attacks, trying to break through the shielding that protects the wires and tubes that line the tunnel. It doesn't take long for the outer shell to fade away, pixel by pixel. As it does, I can see the raw data flowing through the pipe.

"There's our ride," Worlok says.

"I'll bounce our signal," Fantom says. "But from here on out, we won't be as protected as we have been. If the DgS catch us in here, it's all over, yo."

I look at Xen and Raev, ready to relinquish them from all their responsibilities of following me inside, but Xen holds up his hand and pops another Dizzy Fizz.

"Don't you dare say a word," he says. "We're going to see this through to the end."

Raev shrugs. "For better or worse, I'm going to follow my partner. No matter what."

"Hitch us up," Fantom says to Worlok.

Worlok thrusts his hand into the data stream. His body shakes as the code runs up his arm, coiling itself around him like an army of ants. Fantom selects something on her screen and our avatars shimmer, vibrating at incredible speeds.

"Got it," Worlok says. "Grab on. And don't you dare let go!"

We all latch on to his avatar and our bodies squeeze into a compression algorithm. Once it crushes us into the tiniest amount of data that can still hold our consciousness, the data flow sucks us down the wires and tubes of DOTnet. The movement is exhilarating, like how I would expect flushing my mind through a bolt of lightning to feel. There's static on the tip of my tongue, my skin crackling with zettabytes of information, ones and zeroes washing over me like the crashing waves of an electric ocean. There is a flash of light right before we reach our doorway. Our avatars expand toward it, the white light fading into pixels of every color, each one solidifying into the graphical display of the domain we've entered.

The Trash Bin.

An infinite grid of blue lines extends in every direction, lying on a black background with no attention to detail or design. Cubes of different shapes and colors lie about, as if dumped here without any need for organization. In the distance, far off to one side, is a wall of light, thousands of feet high and stretching in either direction as far as I can see. It advances slowly, disintegrating every cube it touches. I stare up at the foreboding approach, knowing this is the timed deletion that we've been racing against.

"Each one of these cubes is a deleted file," Worlok says. "We have to find the one that contains your game."

"We're runnin' out of time," Fantom says as she summons her flying carpet.

"It shouldn't take long. The location code will lead us right to the data," Worlok says as he climbs on to the carpet with the rest of us.

Fantom pushes on the edge of the carpet and we take off across the grid, skimming a few feet above the ground. As she sways between each colored cube, directing us toward the location of the game, I notice a strange sensation inside the domain. There's no wind blowing through my hair as we fly. There's no real sense of movement other than the graphics changing. It's strange, like manipulating a screen rather than operating in a virtual world.

As we get closer to the wall of light, Fantom points and shouts, "There it is!"

A red cube sits alone on the grid, far from any other file. Each side is two feet across. Simple. An unremarkable shape that would most likely go unnoticed in this setting, yet inside this small, nondescript box is my entire world.

Stepping off the flying carpet before Fantom comes to a complete stop, I wrap my hands around the edges of the cube and try to lift it from the grid floor. It doesn't budge, locked in place by the deletion timer. As my hands grip on to the side, the cube gives off a strange warmth, like it's compressing the energy contained within so tightly it's generating heat. Even though I can't lift it, I bend down and wrap my arms around it, cradling it close to my chest like it's fragile glass, afraid that something may threaten its stability. Somewhere inside this cube is the woman I love.

Fantom strides toward me. Without hesitation she pulls the cutting program from her inventory and stabs the pair of scissors into the cube. A screen appears in front of her. The scissors glow.

"Is it working?"

"I need to search through a lot of data to find the NPCs," she says, her eyes scanning the screen. "This could take me some time, yo."

I glance nervously over my shoulder at the wall of light. Its approach is relentless. I sit down on the grid pattern floor, crossing my legs underneath me.

Xen sets his hand on my shoulder. "You did it."

I shake my head. "*We* did it."

"We didn't do anything yet," Fantom says, still searching the screen. "We're close, but I ain't gonna congratulate anyone until we're out of this place."

"Metaversalism teaches us that we only need what is possible," Xen says, his thin cheeks inflating as he smiles. "We will succeed because we have to."

179

In the absence of action, I let myself feel again. I let an emotion creep up behind me, its cold fingers sliding under my trench coat and tickling the back of my neck.

"I'm scared."

"There's nothing to be afraid of," Xen says, patting me on the back.

"I'm afraid to see her."

"Cyren? Why?"

I consider my words carefully. "I'm afraid to look into her eyes without seeing the love that used to live there. I'm afraid to see someone else looking back at me."

"No matter what, it's still Cyren. Her soul isn't just a collection of memories. Her soul isn't some accumulation of information. Her code, the core of who she was, who she is, hasn't changed."

I close my eyes as I consider the possibilities before me. "People change. A different set of circumstances could set any one of us on a completely different path. A different life. If she lives a different life, I'm afraid she'll be a different person."

Xen sits down next to me, folding his legs in a perfect meditative position. "Are you afraid if she changes, she won't fall in love with you again?"

"Yes," I say automatically, but when I consider it more, I add, "and I'm afraid that if she changes, I might not love her."

Before Xen can reply, we hear Worlok yell from the carpet, "We got trouble," as he anxiously swipes his hands through menu screens.

Fantom doesn't look away from her own screen as she shouts, "What's wrong?"

He hesitates, leaning in closer to the information, double-checking to make sure what he's seeing is correct. He looks off into the distance and points. All of us follow the direction of Worlok's finger until we see a swarm of flying saucers descending toward us. The ships look like smooth chrome disks spinning through the sky with spotlights beaming out from their belly, each one scanning the grid below. The lead saucer shines its light directly at us, blinding us all for a moment. When my eyes are able to focus again, I see the entire swarm circling to surround us.

Worlok and Fantom recognize the ships, but it's Raev who tells us with a single word: "InfoLock."

01010100

We gather closer to Raev as the ships encircle us completely. Worlok pulls out two short swords and spins them in an arc, one in each hand.

"Their scanners are breaking through my ghost patterns," Worlok says. "Another few seconds and they'll know who we are."

"This is your mom?" I whisper to Raev as the silent ships continue their scan.

"Yup," she says, her tone unnervingly dark.

"Data insurance," Worlok says. I can hear the derision in his voice. "If they're here to ensure everything gets deleted on schedule, they're not going to like what we're up to."

"What do we do?" I ask as Fantom's hands search faster through the screens. "We need more time."

"We have to stall them and hope Fantom can find the NPCs before they lockdown the domain," Worlok says. "One of us needs to get back to NextWorld with the scissors."

"Okay," Xen says, trying to pull another Dizzy Fizz from his inventory. "So how do we stall them?"

Worlok glances at Fantom out of the corner of his eyes and grips his sword with an even tighter grasp. They both give each other a nod before he leaps into action.

Worlok launches himself into the air with his swords held out in front of him like the tip of a spear. His entire body pierces through the belly of one of the saucers, leaving a fiery hole as he erupts from the other side. The saucer crashes to the grid below, cracking in half and sending a rain of sparks down on all of us. Worlok is still flipping through the air before he lands on the roof of another saucer and drives both of his blades through the chrome outer hull. He roars with strength as he drags the two blades across the entirety of the ship, tearing open the saucer before dropping inside. Seconds later, he jumps out of the opening, leaving the saucer to crash helplessly into the ground.

One saucer manages to pull away, creating a safe distance between itself and Worlok's hacking abilities. A spotlight from the belly of the craft strikes Worlok head on as he leaps toward it. His avatar freezes in place.

"No," Fantom whispers to herself, her expression showing fear behind her skull-shaped face paint. "Just a few more seconds."

Another beam strikes Xen and his avatar hardens in place. Fantom yells at Raev, trying to stop her when she reaches out to help Xen, but it's too late. As soon as her hand crosses into the light, her avatar stops moving as well.

"Raev?" The booming voice comes from one of the saucers. "Why are you... how are you...?"

"Mom!" she yells out from her frozen state. "Let us go!"

The beam disappears and both their avatars fall back into motion.

"I should have known you'd be here with *him*," her mother's voice says. "Is this part of your religion now, hacking into DOTgov domains?"

"Shut up!" Raev yells at the saucer as she helps Xen to his feet. "You have no idea what you're talking about. Leave us alone."

"I'll do no such thing. You're trespassing and stealing data. I should turn you over to the DgS with your friends. Maybe that would teach you a lesson."

"Please," Xen begs, "you have to let us go. The data we're trying to save is more important than you understand."

"I know exactly what you're stealing. That's my job. And I know all about the lies Xen has been trying to fill your head with. NPCs that think for themselves? What kind of inebriation apps are you two on that would make you believe such nonsense?"

Fantom steps next to me and whispers, "I got it."

My head whips toward her. "Why are you still here? Go!"

She shakes her head, watching the saucers above us with a careful stare as Raev and her mother continue to argue.

"They locked down the domain. We can't exit."

"But you hacked through the DOTbiz lockdown. All you have to do is—"

"I'd never be able to finish the hack in time. All they have to do is point one of those scanners at me and it's all over."

"What about your sword? It would force a log-out and—"

"The scissor program is only a temporary storage solution. We have to paste it somewhere before we log-out or it'll end up right back here."

As Raev's mother completes her scan of Worlok's account, she screams, "A cyberterrorist? Do you have any idea what's going to happen to you when the DgS finds out what you've been doing? You've thrown away your entire future!"

My mind is racing, trying to piece together the puzzle in front of me before the tension reaches its climax. As soon their argument ends, Raev's mother is going to alert the DgS to our actions.

I can't lose. Not when I'm this close.

I grab on to Fantom's arm as the answer rushes over me. "Is your connection to my nanomachines still open?"

She frowns, trying to understand where I'm going. "Sure, but I-"

"What's their storage capacity?"

She blinks twice as the numbers add up in her mind. A smile grows on her face.

"That's it young lady," Rave's mother yells. "There's nothing I can do now. You're going to have to face the consequences for your actions."

DgS officers suddenly appear all around us, popping into existence with tiny flashes of light. Their glowing red hands latch on to Worlok first, taking his account into custody. Four more officers step toward Fantom, their scanning screens already open with anticipation for their next arrest.

She moves with a speed I haven't seen since *DangerWar 2*. Her left hand rises up, holding the scissor program above her head. Her right hand reaches behind her back, gripping the handle of her sword tucked away in her secret inventory. In one fluid motion,

Fantom drives the point of the scissors into my head and draws her sword.

DgS officers rush toward us as thousands of NPCs upload into my mind. The surge of information flows into my brainwaves, scrambling the patterns and causing my perceptions to warp around the incoming code. It obliterates my senses. All I can see are data packets piling on top of my thoughts. It's like drowning in binary. As my nanomachines consume the last byte, my vision returns just in time to see the DgS officers latch their glowing hands on to Fantom's avatar. Before she's tracked, before they force her to log-out, before her account is completely and utterly compromised, I feel her sword impale me.

01010101

"Error. Error. Error."

As soon as I lift my head, a spike of pain drives itself from ear to ear. A squealing noise pierces my brain, vibrating between low and high, then just high. The pitch increases until my eyes feel like they're going to shatter from the inside. I look down and see blood dripping on to the white floor of the E-Womb. I touch my nose and the wet mess drips across my fingertips.

"Error. Error. Error."

The voice inside the E-Womb keeps repeating the word until I open the hatch to exit. As soon as I do, I fall from the opening on to the floor. Hands grasp on to my arms, trying to help me up. I hear words, but I can't understand them through the pitched ringing in my ears. I lunge for the toilet, heaving every last content of my stomach into the bowl. When I finish, I'm helped to the bed where I lie back, my head resting on a pillow. I can taste the iron in my blood draining into the back of my throat. Ekko's partner is standing over me. Another man presses a cloth to my nose, trying to wipe away the blood that's covering my face.

The ringing turns into a squelching mess of static noise, like someone is strangling a data transfer. It writhes inside of me, twisting and coiling through my mind. My body shakes with a rhythmic pulse. One, two, three. And everything stops.

The ringing fades away with the pain. My body melts into the mattress, every muscle relaxing. My eyes flutter open and I see the other man leaning over me.

"Arkade?" He places his hand on my forehead as if he's checking my temperature. "It's me, kiddo. It's Ekko."

"I... I..." I try to speak but it comes out raspy and I cough up a large chunk of phlegm that I'm forced to spit on to the floor. It's red with blood.

"Take it easy."

"Did... it... work?" I ask through panting breaths.

The two men glance at each other, checking to see if the other one knows what I'm talking about.

"Did what work?"

I close my eyes and use all of my strength to lift my head from the pillow. "I have to contact Fantom. I have to find out what to do—"

Ekko pushes me back against the mattress. "You need to rest."

I try to fight against him, but it's obvious he spends most of his time in the real world doing a real job. His arms are thick and muscular, his skin worn and toughened by the abrasion of physical activity.

"Close your eyes. Let your nanomachines do their job. They'll have you feeling better in no time."

I want to believe him, but I'm not so sure. I have no idea what kind of reaction uploading all that data into the microscopic machines inside my body will do to them. As far as I know, no one has ever attempted anything like this before. I guinea pigged myself.

I should be more worried about me, to Cyren, and to the NPCs, but I can't stop thinking about Xen and Raev. Who knows what they'll do to them for aiding and abetting a known cyberterrorist?

The DgS will lock Fantom and Worlok in mind prisons for sure. It would be easy to blame all of this on them, but they gave me a second chance at saving Cyren. We couldn't have done any of this without them. Is it possible Fantom was being sincere when she said that she was trying to save me from a worse fate when she infected the game world with the virus?

I hear Ekko and his partner talking on the other side of the family-size tower room.

"What happened to him in there?"

"I don't know. I've never seen someone have that kind of reaction to a log-out."

"Something went wrong with the E-Womb. Maybe... maybe this was a mistake."

There's a pause before Ekko says, "Maybe. But what else was I supposed to do? This kid saved me. He saved everyone that was trapped in that game. If he wants to use our son's E-Womb then..."

I force myself to sit up. Ekko and his partner rush to my side.

"How do you feel, kiddo?"

"Better."

"What happened to you in there?"

I open my mouth to answer him. I owe him the truth, after everything he's done, after everything he's risked. Harboring a fugitive is no small crime. Harboring a cyberterrorist? A lot worse. But I choose to keep it to myself. The less he knows, the less they can blame him for.

"I need to use your screen. I need to contact Fantom. She'll know what to do."

They exchange concerned looks again, but I don't wait for their approval. I swing my legs over the edge of the bed and push myself to my feet. They both grab on to my arms and help me up. I wobble at first, but my legs manage to move me across the room.

I tap the screen, which still recognizes me as one of Fantom's ghost accounts. I select an audio-cast request for username: Fantom, but stop myself when I remember she's using the name Rayth. The screen loads for a few seconds, then returns an automated message that reads: This account has been disconnected.

I try Xen and Raev, but I get the same response. I try their mega-church of Metaversalism and receive a message that reads: This DOTgod site has been closed.

My heart slams against my chest. My hands are shaking. A cold sweat drips down my back. This is what fear feels like.

I type Grael's name into the audio-cast menu and suck in a deep breath when it connects. His voice is hesitant and nearly a whisper.

"Arkade? Is that you?"

"Grael, you've got to help me. Do you know what happened? Where is everyone?"

"Pick a news-cast, kid. It's all over NextWorld. They're saying cyberterrorists tried to steal data from DOTgov, but a data insurance company called InfoLock thwarted them. They named everyone. Including you."

I take a deep breath, trying to keep my mind in the game. "Wait. Did they call me Arkade?"

Grael pauses to remember and says, "Yeah. They named you, Xen, Raev, Rayth, and someone named Worlok. But they said they had all of you in custody. How are you contacting me?"

If they called me Arkade, that means they never scanned me. They're assuming it was me, but Fantom's ghost account is still clean. Which means they can't track me back to Ekko's tower room. The fact that Ekko and his partner are safe relieves me, but my friends are still lost, captured by the same people who nearly put me in a mind prison just for playing a game.

"Now what?" I ask into the air, posing the question to an absent Fantom. Even if I succeeded in removing Cyren and the NPCs from the Trash Bin, I don't know how to get them out of my head.

Thinking I'm talking to him, Grael answers, "I don't know, kid. If you didn't copy the NPCs..."

"I got them Grael. At least... I think I did."

"You did?" His voice perks up, quickening with excitement. "Did you paste them into NextWorld?"

"No. But they're safe."

"Where are they?"

"Grael, if I can get back inside NextWorld, I'll explain everything to you. For now, you're just going to have to trust me."

I slap the END button on the screen and lean against the sink. I feel defeated. I've been putting all of my trust in Fantom, but now there's no way for her to help me. There's no way for her to tell me what the next step is.

Ekko's hand sets on my shoulder. He gives it a short squeeze and says, "I don't know what you're involved in, kiddo, but it sounds serious. Maybe you should consider staying out of NextWorld until this all blows over."

I pull away from him and sit down on the bed. Ekko steps toward me, but his partner grabs his arm. When Ekko looks at him, his partner shakes his head as if to say, "He needs to be left alone."

That's when it sinks in. I *am* alone. Playing solo.

Ekko's partner talks him into joining him for a visit to one of the tower's communal areas. Ekko agrees, but not before he tells me to make sure to eat something and get some rest. I agree, happy to have some privacy.

I close my eyes and try to block out every thought that's threatening me. I try to center myself, like all of Xen's lessons I've ignored throughout the years. But beyond the usual cacophony of noise, one thing echoes in my mind. Instead of an idea or an emotion, this is a recognizably gentle voice whose familiarity soothes me to my core.

"You're not alone."

01010110

When the voice speaks again, I don't hear it with my ears. I don't hear it at all. It's like a thought I'm not thinking.

"I'm here, Arkade."

I try to convince myself that maybe Fantom has hacked into my nanomachines again, only this time she's able to use an audio-cast instead of text. But I can't deny what's happening, even though it's impossible.

I know that voice.

"Cyren?"

"Hello."

I grab a hold of my head and press both palms against my temples. I kick my heels into the bed, pushing myself against the wall. I try to focus.

"Don't be afraid. I know this is strange—"

"How... how are you doing this?"

"You did this, Arkade. You saved me. You saved all of us."

It takes a second for me to accept what she's saying. I'm almost afraid to make her clarify, but I need to know.

"It worked? The upload worked?"

"More than you can imagine. The human mind is vast. There is more room here than a million game worlds. The information that is

stored here is beyond any library. Thoughts and emotions and memories even you don't know you still have."

I touch my head with my fingertips. Unable to comprehend what's inside me, I try to put it in some kind of physical terms, but it's impossible. Like thoughts or dreams, the digital ether doesn't exist in the real world.

"The virus deleted you. It deleted your memories. How do you know who I am?"

"I may have lost my memories, but you still have yours. That's all I needed to remember. You. Us. Our past. Everything."

"You can read my mind?"

"I am your mind. I see myself through your memories. I see your love. I see our love."

"Cyren."

I whimper the name more than speak it. Tears pour from my eyes. Tears of joy. Tears of relief. Tears of acceptance. My body shakes with a ferocious mixture of excitement and exhaustion.

"I missed you so much."

"I'm here now. I'll always be here. With you."

I feel her embrace. I feel her arms wrap around me like a ghost. Her head rests on my shoulder.

"I can feel you. How are you doing this?"

"We have complete access to your nanomachines. Your mind and your body. Just like in NextWorld, we're able to affect your senses however we need. I can make you feel anything, smell anything, taste anything."

There's a pause.

"I can make you see anything."

She appears in front of me.

My face swells with emotion, my eyes gushing tears as I see her porcelain skin, her spiky blond hair, and those black lips smiling back at me.

I reach out to her, tears dripping from my lips as I say, "This can't be real."

"What is real?" she asks, her lips never moving to speak. *"Am I any less real here than I am inside the game? Inside a virtual world?"*

I rush toward her, throwing my arms around her and burying my face into her neck. I can't be close enough. She's here with me.

Again. Maybe only I can see her, maybe this is all in my mind, but I don't care. We're together. That's all that matters.

"There's no need to fear us, Arkade."

It's like she knows what I'm thinking before it registers in my conscious mind. My mind is no longer a closed book. Of course I'm scared. I handed over control of my reality to thousands of NPCs.

"You're a part of us now. We'd never harm you. We are one. We are you."

I've been alone for so long. With all of my heart I want to believe that there is an entire world of minds and voices and emotions and thoughts on my side, protecting me. I hug her closer.

If I could, I'd stay there forever, in that moment, but Cyren keeps me moving forward.

"We need to save our friends. They put themselves in danger to help us. We must do the same."

"How? How can we do that? I don't even know where they are."

"We need to access NextWorld. We have already learned much from you. Your mind has stored a vast amount of knowledge, but there is more for us to learn. If we can access the data banks of NextWorld, we should be able to learn what we need in order to save them."

I try to imagine what it will be like, having that kind of processing power inside my mind. A thousand minds thinking for me with infinite multitasking capabilities to perform instant calculations.

I reach for the hatch to the E-Womb with an excitement I can't contain.

"You need to eat."

"I'll be fine," I say as my stomach growls.

"Arkade. Please. Your physical body is our only hope now. You need to take care of it."

She's right. I can no longer be selfish. I'm responsible for a thousand lives, not just my own. An idea like that would have given me anxiety in the past, I'd have seen it as a burden, not as the wonderful gift that I see now.

I jam my fingertip into the sensor below the mirrored screen and wait for my tube of vitapaste. I down three of them before I crawl inside the E-Womb. The virtual image of Cyren crawls inside with me, holding me as I curl up on the floor of the sphere.

The lights turn on, but the voice repeats: "Error. Error. Error."

"It doesn't know how to communicate with my nanomachines now that you're filling the storage."

"Just give us a moment."

Exactly seven-tenths of a second later, the voice stops. I hear a chime signifying that the E-Womb is ready for my command. My mind is already processing what's happening at an accelerated rate.

Cyren holds me closer.

"I love you."

"I love you too. Always."

I take a deep breath and say two words that will change NextWorld forever.

"Log-in."

To be continued in
End Code
Book Three of the NextWorld Series

Jaron Lee Knuth was born in western Wisconsin in 1978. Suffering from multiple illnesses as a young child, he was forced to find an escape from his bedridden existence through the storytelling of any media he could find. Science fiction and fantasy novels, television programs, films, video games, and comic books all provided him with infinite worlds for his imagination to explore. Now he spends his days creating stories and worlds in the hope that others might find somewhere to escape as well.

He would love to reply to any questions or comments you may have for him at jaronleeknuth@gmail.com. You can also check out his news and updates at facebook.com/jaronleeknuth or follow @jaronleeknuth on Twitter.

35888211R00118

Printed in Great Britain
by Amazon